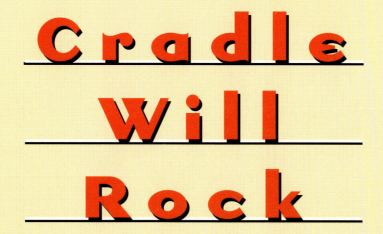

Cradle Will Rock

Cradle Will Rock

The Movie and The Moment

Tim Robbins

Includes dialogue and lyrics from
Marc Blitzstein's *The Cradle Will Rock*

Foreword by Paul Newman

Historical notes by Eric Darton and
Nancy Stearns Bercaw; additional
contributions by Robert Tracy

Edited by Theresa Burns   Designed by Timothy Shaner

A Newmarket Press Pictorial Moviebook

NEWMARKET PRESS
New York

SS, EMLA
JHR, MGR

First Edition

1 3 5 7 9 10 8 6 4 2

Library of Congress Cataloging-in-Publication Data

Robbins, Tim.
Cradle will rock: the movie and the moment/Tim Robbins. Includes dialogue and lyrics from
Marc Blitzstein's *The Cradle Will Rock*; foreword by Paul Newman; historical notes by Eric Darton
and Nancy Stearns Bercaw; additional contributions by Robert Tracy; edited by Theresa Burns.
p. cm.
1. Cradle will rock (Motion picture) I. Burns, Theresa. II. Title.

PN1997.C848 R63 1999
791.43'72—dc 21   99-052093

ISBN 1-55704-399-X

QUANTITY PURCHASES
Companies, professional groups, clubs, and other organizations may qualify for special
terms when ordering quantities of this title. For information, write Special Sales,
Newmarket Press, 18 East 48th Street, New York, NY 10017; call (212) 832-3575;
fax (212) 832-3629; or e-mail newmktprs@aol.com.

www.newmarketpress.com

Manufactured in the United States of America.

Cradle Will Rock

Contents

Foreword

by Paul Newman

When I arrived in New York in 1951, the Federal Theatre had been extinct for many years, but its memory and inspirations were still present, echoing in the halls of the Music Box Theatre and in the backstage dressing rooms. I didn't give it much thought at the time—as a young actor starting out I was looking toward the future and not the past. But the Federal Theatre influenced me as it did every young actor at the time, whether we were aware of it or not.

Coming out of the Depression, the theatre community was given a much-needed boost by the FTP. Older theatre professionals were reinvigorated by the program, while young, unpublished playwrights were inspired by the daring productions they saw staged. One of Tennessee Williams's first plays, *Not About Nightingales,* was originally submitted as a Living Newspaper for the Federal Theatre. The play, an exposé of corrupt and cruel prison policies based on newspaper accounts of the time, was recently unearthed by actress Vanessa Redgrave and given its Broadway premiere last year. Arthur Miller—himself a young audience member of Federal Theatre shows—went on to a pretty decent career of his own. And Elia Kazan, who as a director was able to elevate the art of acting, ironically also had his start in the socially conscious theatre of Hallie Flanagan. Who else? Joe Losey, Elmer Rice, Orson Welles, John Houseman, John Randolph, Joe Cotten, Burt Lancaster, Arlene Francis, Sidney Lumet. The Federal Theatre forged a new ground, plowed the soil, and left it fertile and ready for greenhorns like me to sow our seeds and watch a brand-new crop flower. The theatre of New York in the fifties burst through years of tradition and delivered a potent and ultimately liberating emotional release. Themes long held to be taboo were explored, the authority of our collective patriarchy was questioned, and out of the chaos and tailspin that resulted came a decade of exciting and groundbreaking work. The courage to explore this new ground had its roots in the Federal Theatre.

But Tim Robbins's new movie is not just about the theatre. One needn't have passed through an education in drama to appreciate it. It's about so much more—power and corruption, freedom of expression, the rise of Fascism, the beginnings of the Red hunt, the connection between money and art, the simple dreams of a young actress, the tragedy of the fading vaudevillian—all done at the dizzying pace of a screwball comedy. Themes of the prostitution of one's profession, of government censorship of the arts, of the ability of the common man to rise to extraordinary acts of courage, all resonate today in the movie as they did in the thirties. The film, and now this book, brings us into this world as if it were our own, never painting the past as distant or remote. Instead, they link us to the past as a living thing, as interconnected and alive as all of our collective stories, or histories, should be.

Hope you enjoy.

The Movie and
The Moment

by Tim Robbins

I have a lot of faith in audiences.

For every destructive and negative impulse catered
to by certain moviemakers, I believe there are audiences who want more, who are desperate for positive
reflections of humanity. When I initially heard the
true story of the first performance of *The Cradle Will
Rock*, my immediate reaction was "What an ending
for a film." Here was a positive, uplifting celebration
of humanity, creativity, and freedom. What amazing
courage it must have taken for those actors to rise
from their seats.

I'm inspired by dangerous art. To understand the
impact and thrill of that first performance of *Cradle*
one really has to understand the tenor of the times.
So in filling the spaces in the script that led up to
the performance, I had the responsibility of creating
an accurate portrayal of 1930s New York—that is,
what was happening economically, socially, and
politically. At the same time, I wanted to avoid
the boring tone of a history lesson. I realized that
while it was essential to get to the central themes
of politics and hunger, Fascism versus Communism,
etcetera, I also needed to find a spirit of fun and
humor that could lift the film and carry it along with
a certain speed and pace. I drew my stylistic inspiration from the thirties' screwball comedies of Preston

Sturges, Frank Capra, and Howard Hawks. I knew that in order to pull it off, pace was key and humor was essential. It was also necessary to portray characters who were forced to face the difficult decisions of the time, characters confronted with hunger and desperation. Through these individuals, we hoped to portray the noble humanity and courage of those who endured the Depression. And finally, I wanted to present an alternate account of the actions of the ruling classes, pre–World War II. In the entire pantheon of films depicting that war, I don't believe we have ever been given an indication of the American business and government complicity in the rise of the European war machines.

Imagine this: For your entire life, you have put your faith in the capitalist system. Then, one October day in 1929 the stock market crashes. Despite the fact that you have never invested in the stock market, you are told that this affects you. And it does. In a matter of weeks, your local bank has failed. Your money is gone. Your small business fails. You are laid off. Unemployed and with no prospects, you are asked to be patient and continue to believe in this system of government that has left you bankrupt, jobless, and hungry. You—a hard-working, God-fearing person who has done nothing wrong—stand on long lines with your family just to get a bite to eat.

Then along comes someone from the Communist Party. "We believe in the redistribution of wealth," they say, "that everyone is equal. Look how your capitalism has failed you. Join with us."

This way of thinking met with a lot of open ears. There was a real and tangible fear within the corridors of power that our system of

Unemployment lines, like these at the WPA offices, were common in the Depression.

government could collapse. I truly believe that the Roosevelt administration saved democracy in our country. The New Deal put people back to work and restored their faith in the government. But strangely, the elite classes and big business hated Roosevelt and despised the New Deal. Indeed, many of the strong and powerful in our society believed Roosevelt to be a Communist and would have dismantled every alphabet agency in existence if given the chance.

Robbins, with assistant director Allan Nicholls, discusses the labor rally in Madison Square.

Many prominent business leaders in America saw an alternative to Roosevelt's policies in the Fascist governments of Europe. In Italy, dealing with his own economic crisis, Mussolini made the trains run on time. He had a strong, efficient government. Hitler turned around the German economy and put people back to work. And Franco was fighting a war against the Communists in Spain. Our corporate leaders and press magnates thought this was great, and supported these administrations with trade and raw materials. William Randolph Hearst ran a weekly column in Mussolini's name (ghostwritten by Margherita Sarfatti) in his newspapers. American citizens who protested the loss of civil liberties in Germany and the expansionist policies of Italy in Ethiopia were labeled Communists. Meanwhile, the labor movement was gaining power in the United States, which added fuel to the fire and convinced business leaders that Moscow was not only knocking on the door, but was already in the house. It was within this volatile world that *Cradle*—as well as the Rivera mural and other Federal Theatre productions—needed to be placed. In the minds of those in power, these were not just works of art; they were dangerous subversions whose express purpose was the overthrow of the social order.

Before I started writing the screenplay, I read *Arena*, Hallie Flanagan's account of the Federal Theatre. Having been a theatre major in college, I was shocked that I'd never learned of this amazing achievement. The avenues it would open in students' minds could lead to such possibilities. Here was an arts administrator who not only embraced the great playwrights of the past, but encouraged brand new forms of expression—she was excited by experimental theatre, Russian constructivism, fresh interpretations of classics, modern dance, puppetry, and vibrant children's theatre. Under the Federal Theatre, touring companies brought shows into hardscrabble rural areas; vaudeville was rediscovered and reenergized; religious pageants, circus shows, and historical dramas specific to the area in which they were performed were presented; and a brand new form of theatre, the Living Newspaper, was invented, nurtured, and brought to life.

The plays that were social in nature, that created the most trouble with Congress, were some of the biggest hits, meaning of course that there was a strong desire on the part of the public to see them. The Federal Theatre was creating plays that made people think, question. Yet, ironically, those plays represented only 10 percent of the agency's output—the great majority of productions were not social or political in nature.

Hallie Flanagan's accomplishments were astonishing. I don't think there is any way to measure the effect the Federal Theatre had on this nation. When you consider that the project reached 25 million people, or about a quarter of the U.S. population, you begin to get a sense of its impact. How many spirits were lifted temporarily from the hard-core poverty of the Depression, how many imaginations were ignited, how many outcasts in small towns saw these weird actors passing through town and felt better about themselves, perhaps even found their way into theatre careers of their own? The much-needed laughter, the emotions shared, the spectacles, the puppet shows, the social dramas—all were provided free or at affordable prices by Uncle Sam.

Re-creating the Welles-Houseman production of Faustus, *a highlight of the Federal Theatre.*

Live theatre is a burning fuel. I can still remember productions I saw as a youth. Specifics fade but the moments of magic, of elegiac beauty, of fierce passion, of striking set designs, explosions, metamorphic performances, grace, pain— these moments linger in my subconscious and are revisited again and again when I'm trying to create. How many moments of creativity, how many plays, poems, and songs were inspired over the years by the Federal Theatre? Its true legacy is immeasurable. It is a legacy of millions of laughs, millions of creative fires lit, millions of elevations of the human spirit—perhaps our government's most radical and most culturally uplifting achievement.

Cradle Will Rock

Principal Cast

HANK AZARIA
as Marc Blitzstein

RUBEN BLADES
as Diego Rivera

JOAN CUSACK
as Hazel Huffman

JOHN CUSACK
as Nelson Rockefeller

CARY ELWES
as John Houseman

PHILIP BAKER HALL
as Gray Mathers

CHERRY JONES
as Hallie Flanagan

ANGUS MACFADYEN
as Orson Welles

BILL MURRAY
as Tommy Crickshaw

VANESSA REDGRAVE
as Countess La Grange

SUSAN SARANDON
as Margherita Sarfatti

JAMEY SHERIDAN
as John Adair

JOHN TURTURRO
as Aldo Silvano

EMILY WATSON
as Olive Stanton

BARBARA SUKOWA
as Sophie Silvano

BOB BALABAN
as Harry Hopkins

JACK BLACK and KYLE GASS
as Sid and Larry

PAUL GIAMATTI
as Carlo

HARRIS YULIN
as Chairman Martin Dies

GIL ROBBINS
as Congressman Starnes

JOHN CARPENTER
as William Randolph Hearst

GRETCHEN MOL
as Marion Davies

VICTORIA CLARK
as Dulce Fox

BARNARD HUGHES
as Frank Marvel

TIMOTHY JEROME
as Bert Weston

HENRY STRAM
as Hiram Sherman

CHRIS McKINNEY
as Canada Lee

ERIN HILL
as Sandra Mescal

DANIEL JENKINS
as Will Geer

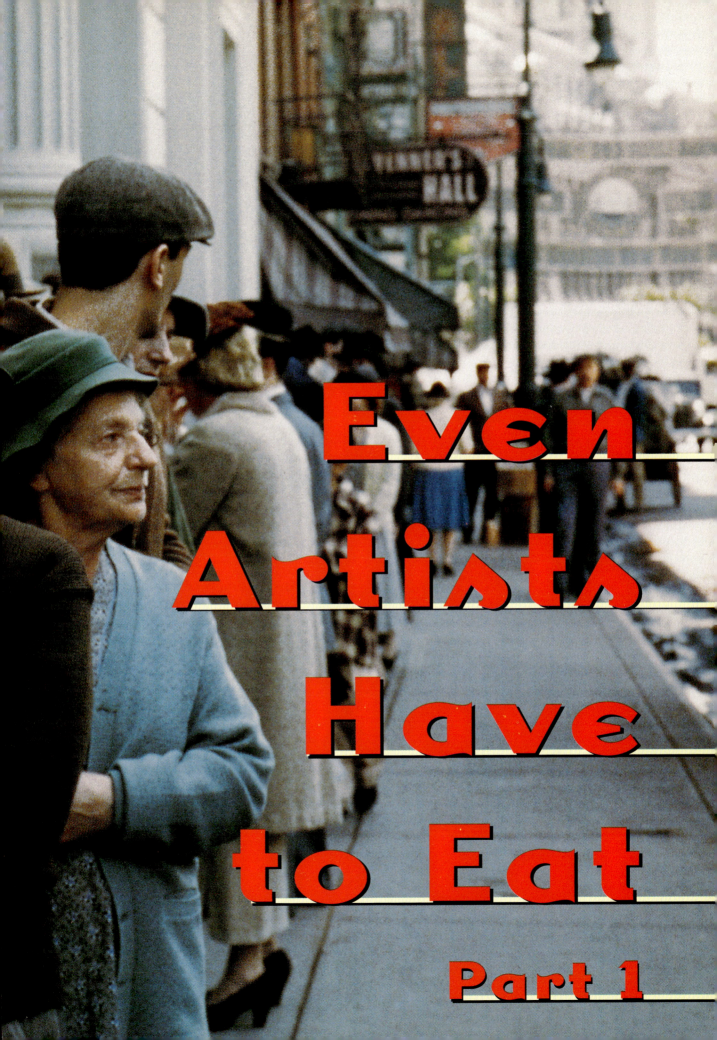

Even Artists Have to Eat

Part 1

Title: NEW YORK, FALL 1936

INT. MOVIE THEATRE. DAWN.

Olive Stanton, a young girl in her early twenties, skinny, waiflike, with eyes of hope, slowly wakes up. We pull out to see that her blanket is actually a curtain, a red velvet theatrical curtain. She awakes from the noise of a running projector and leaves the theatre as a worker approaches. A newsreel plays. Olive moves quickly out of a side stage door and into an alley.

EXT. STREET. DAWN.

Olive stops at the end of the alley and squats to relieve herself. The camera finds Hazel Huffman, a fiercely committed woman in her thirties, attaching a leaflet to a bulletin board. As she moves on we change directions, following a well-dressed man, who brings us back to Olive.

> OLIVE
> Song for a nickel, mister.

> MAN
> What?

> OLIVE
> I'll sing you a song for a nickel.

> MAN
> No, thank you.

He moves on. We follow Olive down the street. She hums a popular tune from the day. The camera cranes up to find:

INT. BLITZSTEIN APARTMENT. DAWN.

Marc Blitzstein, twenty-eight years old, with a wild look in his eyes, is seated at his piano, composing.

> BLITZSTEIN *(singing)*
> I AIN'T IN STEELTOWN LONG,
> I WORK TWO DAYS A WEEK;
> THE OTHER FIVE MY EFFORTS
>   AIN'T REQUIRED.

A woman's voice (Moll) joins him, and his fades away. As the voice is heard we move in on the sheet music and Blitzstein's hand writing the notes and words.

> MOLL *(singing)*
> FOR TWO DAYS OUT OF SEVEN,
> TWO DOLLAR BILLS I'M GIVEN.

Close-up Blitzstein. Then we see a toy theatre on top of the piano. A small female character center stage.

> MOLL *(singing)*
> SO I'M JUST SEARCHING ALONG THE STREET,

Olive Stanton (Emily Watson) wakes up in the theatre under a newsreel featuring Franklin Delano Roosevelt.

FOR ON THOSE FIVE DAYS IT'S NICE TO EAT.
JESUS, JESUS, WHO SAID LET'S EAT?

*Silence, a radio plays "March of Time." Blitzstein listens.
A metronome ticks.*

INT. MATHERS'S MANSION (DINING ROOM). MORNING.
*A radio plays "March of Time." Industrialist, art patron
Gray Mathers sits at an elegantly appointed breakfast table
with his wife, the Countess. An unidentified man with a
handlebar mustache and pretentious air sits chewing.*

MATHERS
Negroes, dear?

COUNTESS
Yes, Negroes.

MATHERS
All Negroes?

COUNTESS
All Negroes, dear.

MATHERS
A minstrel show?

COUNTESS
No dear. *Macbeth.* I said so before. *Macbeth.*
Shakespeare.

MATHERS
With Negroes?

COUNTESS
Yes. Carlo says it's unlucky to say "Macbeth" in
the theater. So what do they call it? What is it,
Carlo?

CARLO
The Scottish play.

COUNTESS
Yes, the Scottish play. But there isn't really
anything Scottish in this production.

MATHERS
I don't know a lot of Negro Scots.

COUNTESS
Oh, Gray, dear. You don't know a lot of Negro
anything. (*A butler brings her the morning newspaper.*) Oh, dear.

MATHERS
I know. I got a call last night.

COUNTESS
It's not you, thank God.

CARLO
What is?

COUNTESS
Labor riots.

Carlo makes a face.

MATHERS
The reception for the Italian exhibit is today
at noon.

COUNTESS
Italian exhibit at noon.

MATHERS
Please don't be late.

COUNTESS
Carlo and I are going to see a theatrical producer
today.

MATHERS
A producer? Why?

COUNTESS
To learn about the artistic process.

MATHERS
The artistic process?

COUNTESS
Yes, the theatrical craft.

MATHERS
What time is the exhibit?

COUNTESS
Noon. I'll be there, darling.

**EXT. STREET OUTSIDE WPA/FED THEATRE OFFICES.
EARLY MORNING.**
*Aldo Silvano, a man in his thirties, walks briskly, holding
the hands of his three children. They are dressed in school
uniforms.*

JOEY
When's Mommy coming home?

SILVANO
In a couple of days. Churn.

CHANCE
C-H-U-R-N.

JOEY
What's the baby's name?

SILVANO
Person.

In the fall of 1929, on the eve of a four-year bull market's astonishing collapse, President Herbert Hoover took to the radio airwaves to assure Americans that "the fundamental business of this country is on a sound and prosperous basis." From his Pocantico Hills estate, John D. Rockefeller issued a public statement affirming that "my son and I have for some days been purchasing sound common stock."

Then on October 24—later to be known as "Black Thursday"—a plunge in Wall Street stock prices triggered a banking panic that in turn prompted a steep, long-term sell-off. At the time, few Americans owned stocks, so most people did not immediately feel the effects of the crash or realize its implications for their future. But within months, industrialized market economies world-wide had effectively melted down.

Unless one has lived through it, a social catastrophe of the length and intensity of the Great Depression is nearly impossible to imagine. But happen it did. Between the October crash and the end of 1929, unemployment in the United States rose from less than half a million to over four million. Soup kitchens and bread lines sprang up in cities everywhere. By the time the market hit bottom, stock values had plummeted from $87 billion to $18 billion, and investment fell by 98 percent. Steel production stood at 12 percent of capacity, and construction ground to a halt. Within a few years, one-third of the labor force would be out of work. So many able-bodied men were selling apples on street corners that the Census Bureau classified them as employed.

Though economically beleaguered, Americans were by no means politically paralyzed. Twenty thousand unemployed World War I veterans converged on the Capitol, and in scores of factories and steel mills workers pressed a militant, often violently repressed struggle that

Production designer Richard Hoover created realistic Depression scenes like this one from actual photographs of the period.

culminated in 1935 with the Wagner Act, guaranteeing workers the right to organize, strike, boycott, and picket. The emergence of the Soviet Union as a world-class industrial power and a prospective "worker's paradise" provided a credible, if illusory, alternate model for economically disenfranchised Americans. Hired by the government to report on social conditions, newspaper-woman Lorena Hickock wrote that "vast numbers of the unemployed are 'right on the edge'—it wouldn't take much to make Communists out of them."

Enter Franklin Delano Roosevelt. His landslide election to the presidency in 1932 marked nothing less than a national referendum on the future of capitalism-as-usual. Roosevelt had called for a New Deal, one in which the federal government shouldered responsibility for alleviating social ills. The most enduring legacy of the Roosevelt era remains the Social Security Act, enacted in 1935 to provide an economic safety net for the elderly. But FDR's policies went far beyond providing a baseline for the country's most vulnerable citizens. In practical terms, the New Deal meant that the government was assuming virtually every function private enterprise had defaulted on—subsidizing and managing the lion's share of the nation's real estate, banking, insurance, electrical power, agricultural and timber production, as well as transport and shipping—until the economy rebounded.

But Roosevelt's recovery strategy brought to crisis proportions the gulf already separating the interests of wealthy Americans from those of the poor, whose numbers now swelled into the tens of millions. Conservative politicians and businessmen bitterly

Danger: America Not Working

Apple sellers in New York, 1930s.

opposed FDR's "socialist" policies, even to the point of challenging their constitutionality in the Supreme Court. To the majority of voters, however, it was clear that only radical reform could prevent the outbreak of open class warfare. That FDR was the only president in U.S. history to serve four terms in the Oval Office testifies both to his personal popularity and to the sense of stability his programs brought to a traumatized nation.

Under Roosevelt's administration, the Herculean task of putting millions back to work and stimulating industrial production fell to dozens of newly created "alphabet agencies," each carrying out a specialized purpose. The hydroelectric projects of the Tennessee Valley Authority (TVA) brought power to the rural South. The Agricultural Adjustment Administration (AAA) subsidized farm prices. The Civilian Conservation Corps (CCC) marshaled an army of young men to build state and national parks.

But the heart of the New Deal was the Works Progress Administration (WPA). Founded in 1935, the WPA was run by Harry Hopkins, a former social worker deeply committed to his agency's mission. "Give a man a dole and you save his body and destroy his spirit," Hopkins often said. "Give him a job and you save both body and spirit."

While the WPA built bridges, highways, dams, national parks, libraries, and hospitals, it also funded the work of writers and visual and performing artists, and brought the fruits of their labor to millions of Americans. The Federal Theatre Project (FTP) was charged with presenting "American life" onstage at a ticket price anyone could afford, while the FTP's sister program, the Federal Art Project (FAP), employed thousands of visual artists— the vast majority of them on relief. When congressional conservatives attacked the leftist content of many of the WPA's cultural projects, Hopkins countered that artists needed "to eat just like other people."

Despite nine years of the New Deal, it took the advent of World War II to fully restore industrial production, absorb all the unemployed, and finally lay the Depression to rest. By 1943 when the WPA was dissolved, it had spent $11 billion providing work and financial aid to 38 million Americans. Among them was the legendary folk balladeer Woody Guthrie. Working under a grant from the WPA, Guthrie traveled to the Pacific Northwest, where the Grand Coulee Dam was being built. Inspired, he wrote one of his most stirring and beautiful songs—an anthem to the fervent hopes embodied in the New Deal. "Roll on Columbia," Guthrie urged the once-wild river. "Your power is turning our darkness to dawn—so roll on Columbia, roll on."

Alongside the building of a modern infrastructure, an American cultural renaissance had flourished in the depths of the Depression.

CHANCE
P-E-R-S-O-N.

JOEY
What's the baby's name?

SILVANO
Antonio. You like it?

We come to Olive waiting on line at WPA talking with an Eastern European man.

MAN
Excuse me, ma'am, is this the line for to get a job?

OLIVE
I think so.

MAN
I'm a carpenter. I work with my hands. It is a good government that wants to build.

OLIVE
Yes.

MAN
I build with wood.

OLIVE
Yes?

The writer of Revolt of the Beavers *pitches the play to Hallie Flanagan (Cherry Jones) outside her offices.*

MAN
What do you do?

OLIVE
This might be the wrong line. This is for theatre. For actors and musicians, I believe.

MAN
You are an actress?

OLIVE
Yes, is this the right line for the Federal Theatre Project?

OLDER MAN
I think this is a line for everything.

OLIVE
Are there other lines?

OLDER MAN
There's other lines inside.

OLIVE
But are there lines for theatre jobs inside?

OLDER MAN
I believe so.

MAN
I'll work anywhere. I'll dig ditches, pour slag, act, it doesn't matter.

We see a man dressed in a colorful costume, rollerskating, who leads us to Hallie Flanagan.

EXT. STREET OUTSIDE WPA/FED THEATRE OFFICES. DAY.
Hallie Flanagan, director of the Federal Theatre, an energetic, sharp-witted woman, walks toward the front door of the building.

> BEAVER MAN
>
> Are you Hallie Flanagan?

> HALLIE
>
> Yes, Mister.

> BEAVER MAN
>
> Beaver, I'm a beaver.

> HALLIE
>
> Beaver. Mr. Beaver, what can I do for you?

> BEAVER MAN
>
> Well, I'm completely embarrassed, but I heard you would be here and I am a playwright and I have written a children's play called *Revolt of the Beavers*. I wonder if you would read my script.

> HALLIE
>
> Absolutely, Mr. Beaver.

Hallie laughs. He gives her the script.

> HALLIE
>
> You have to fill out submission forms.

> BEAVER MAN
>
> I did. All of the information is inside. It's got great music. I'd be happy to play it for you. I'll be right back.

He skates away. We follow Hallie into the building.

INT. WPA OFFICES. DAY.
Tommy Crickshaw, a fifty-year-old vaudevillian, is talking to Rose, Hallie's secretary, as Hallie enters.

> CRICKSHAW
>
> I'm not a teacher. I'm an entertainer.

> HALLIE
>
> What's the problem?

> ROSE
>
> Mr. Crickshaw works at the vaudeville project and he is complaining about the policy there.

> CRICKSHAW
>
> I'm supposed to tutor two no-talents. Impossible.

> HALLIE
>
> Well, Mr. Crickshaw. We were hoping that you

Cherry Jones in the role of Hallie Flanagan: "I was amazed that this woman appeared at just the right time, with all the qualifications needed for something as outrageously ambitious as the FTP. As with any great character, she was full of wonderful contradictions. It was hard to nail her down completely—there's not even an audio tape left of her speaking, this tremendously articulate woman."

would introduce young people to vaudeville, encourage them to take it up, prolong its life.

> CRICKSHAW
>
> Prolong its life? Vaudeville will be around long after you and your Communists are.

> HALLIE
>
> Communists, sir?

> ROSE
>
> Hallie, you have a meeting.

> HALLIE
>
> Mr. Crickshaw.

Crickshaw leaves. Hallie begins to walk upstairs. Rose is following.

INT. FEDERAL THEATRE OFFICES (HALLWAY). DAY.
Hallie and Rose walk briskly.

> ROSE
>
> Two Chinese gentlemen in native dress came by last night, want you to start a Chinese theatre. Very polite. They'll come again. Also you got a call yesterday saying that we can't hire an elephant for the Brooklyn circus.

Free, Adult, Uncensored

As the Depression wore on, the growing popularity of radio, records, and Hollywood movies drastically shrank the demand for live performances. The number one song in 1937—Ira Gershwin's "Nice Work If You Can Get It"—became an ironic mantra for showpeople of all types.

Enter the Federal Theatre Project, a bold initiative of Harry Hopkins's WPA, that along with other "white collar" relief programs for artists and writers, put forty thousand skilled professionals—among them musicians, actors, technicians, stagehands, and costume designers—back to work by the end of its first year in operation.

Bolder still was Hopkins's choice to head the FTP. Hallie Flanagan, a classmate of Hopkins's from Grinnell College and the first woman to be awarded a Guggenheim Fellowship, was a natural trailblazer. She had studied theatre extensively in Europe and the Soviet Union, later distinguishing herself as director of experimental theatre at Vassar College.

With Flanagan, Hopkins could realize his vision of a national theater that was "free, adult, uncensored . . . run by a person who sees right from the start that the profits won't be money profits." As Hopkins told his new appointee, "This is an American job, not just a New York job. It's a job just down your alley." But from the start Hopkins realized that the FTP could serve as a lightning rod for opponents of the WPA, and warned his protégé that "whatever happens, you'll be wrong."

In July 1935, Flanagan hit the ground running, organizing an ambitious mix of new American plays and traditional repertoire that ranged from works by Shakespeare, Molière, Shaw, and O'Neill to the Welles-Houseman adaptation of Marlowe's *Faustus*, and Aristophanes's *Lysistrata*, the latter performed by one of the FTP's sixteen "Negro units." Flanagan also extended the program's original mandate to include children's theatre as well as vaudeville, variety, marionette, and circus performances.

Flanagan's goal was to create theatrical content as innovative, challenging, and high quality as the stark, edgy

> **"From unknown she became anathema: a woman, an amateur, a fanatic armed with millions of the taxpayers' money. . . . Accused alternately of being arty, subversive, and reactionary, an impractical dreamer and an unscrupulous politician, this small, red-haired lady with the firm mouth and the ferocity of a roused tiger was receptive to almost any form of creative theatrical activity."**
>
> —John Houseman, from the Foreword to *Arena*

Center: Hallie Flanagan, Director of the Federal Theatre Project. *"Hallie was a woman like Eleanor Roosevelt. She was that kind of person—nothing like her physically, but the spirit, the soul, the dedication . . . and the drive. It was very much how you felt when you met Eleanor Roosevelt." —Marcella Cisney, radio actress*

The original set of One-Third of a Nation, *which dramatized the need for better housing in the big cities by focusing on slum conditions. "The play fit well within Roosevelt's New Deal policies, although one radical character suggested that the only way slums would vanish was through a redistribution of income."*
—*from* Free, Adult, Uncensored, *edited by John O'Connor and Lorraine Brown*

production values the FTP became known for—a strategy that tested both artistic and political limits. One of her favorite projects was the "Living Newspaper" series, which combined drama straight out of newspaper headlines with calls for social action, harnessing—to the alarm of conservative politicians and business interests—the power of the "well-aimed fact." One Living Newspaper, Arthur Arent's *Power*, was expressly written in support of the public ownership of utilities like the TVA. It was immediately assailed as Communist propaganda.

The high watermark of the FTP saw twenty-eight simultaneous productions of *It Can't Happen Here*—Sinclair Lewis's nightmare vision of a totalitarian coup in America—presented nationwide in several languages and with racially mixed casts. *One-Third of a Nation* (its title taken from a reference to the housing crisis in FDR's second inaugural address) played to standing-room audiences in New York for a year before opening in ten other cities.

In addition to Orson Welles and John Houseman, the FTP served as a talent incubator and launching pad for actors Burt Lancaster, John Huston, Canada Lee, E. G. Marshall, Jack Carter, and Will Geer; screenwriter Dale Wasserman (*One Flew over the Cuckoo's Nest*); and directors Nick Ray (*Rebel Without a Cause*) and Sidney Lumet.

Though the furor over Blitzstein's *Cradle* and other controversial productions provided conservatives with plenty of ammunition, the FTP's greatest vulnerability lay in its split mission. Many politicians who grudgingly supported temporary "relief programs" drew the line at an ongoing national theatre—particularly one whose productions routinely espoused racial equality and the redistribution of wealth. Despite (or perhaps because) its plays were successfully winning mass audiences in thirty-one states, the FTP's political enemies increasingly sharpened their attacks and eventually succeeded in cutting congressional funding in the spring of 1939.

But by the time the curtain rang down on Hallie Flanagan's tumultuous four-year experiment in bringing "American life" onstage, fully one quarter of the public had seen an FTP production. Millions had ventured into a theatre for the first time. And hundreds of thousands more, in remote towns and villages throughout the nation, found to their amazement that American theatre had come to them.

HALLIE
Why not?

ROSE
They're not eligible for relief.

O'Hara approaches.

O'HARA
Hallie. Welcome home. How was your trip?

HALLIE
Great. I've got wonderful things to report.

O'HARA
Did you hear about the elephant?

HALLIE
Not eligible for relief.

O'HARA
Also there's a guy in a squirrel outfit been hanging around trying to see you.

HALLIE
Beaver.

O'HARA
What?

HALLIE
He's a beaver. A playwright.

O'HARA
Oh, playwright.

ROSE
Also there's trouble in Minnesota. Seems an ex fan dancer auditioned for the Federal Theatre there.

HALLIE
Fan dancer?

O'HARA
Burlesque. Takes her clothes off, you know. Anyway, so she auditions. She doesn't get the job but the papers ran the photo of her and said that the Federal Theatre was now employing strippers.

They reach an office where Pierre de Rohan, friend and associate of Hallie, awaits.

HALLIE
Pierre.

DE ROHAN
Hello, darling. I trust you're not too tired from touring the U.S.A.

HALLIE
Oh, Pierre. I have seen such great theatre. So inspiring.

DE ROHAN
Have you heard the rumors?

HALLIE
About the stripper?

DE ROHAN
Stripper. No. People from Washington snooping around our files. There's all this talk about Congressman Dies.

HALLE
Dies as in death?

DE ROHAN
Something about a subcommittee.

HALLIE
No, it's news to me. Hello, everybody.

INT. BLITZSTEIN APARTMENT. DAWN.
Blitzstein paces the floor. He has been up all night. He is singing to his wife, Eva, who has just woken up.

BLITZSTEIN
GO STAND ON SOMEONE'S NECK
WHILE YOU'RE TAKIN';

Countess La Grange (Vanessa Redgrave), her sidekick Carlo (Paul Giamatti), and Augusta Weissberger (Adele Robbins) watch Project 891 rehearse.

CUT INTO SOMEBODY'S THROAT AS YOU PUT—
FOR EVERY DREAM AND SCHEME'S
DEPENDING ON WHETHER,
ALL THROUGH THE STORM,
YOU'VE KEPT IT WARM . . .
THE NICKEL UNDER YOUR FOOT.

EVA
Who's singing?

BLITZSTEIN
A prostitute. She's starving. She sells herself for food. She thinks she feels a nickel under her foot, but when she reaches for it there's nothing there. She's that hungry. You hate that, don't you?

EVA
I didn't say that. I didn't say anything. I'm not here. You haven't slept in two days. Go to sleep.

She disappears. A ghost. A beat. Blitzstein lurches. He exits the apartment.

EXT. MAXINE ELLIOTT'S THEATRE. DAY.
Hazel Huffman attaches a leaflet to the wall, turns to leave, and knocks into Blitzstein walking along. He has a bit of a wild look in his eyes. He needs sleep. He apologizes to Huffman and helps her pick up the leaflets that have scattered about. Tommy Crickshaw picks up one of the scattered leaflets, eyes Hazel, and moves on. We see the Countess and Carlo just getting out of their limousine.

Houseman greets the Countess La Grange and Carlo.

COUNTESS
I thought the play was charming, Jack, utterly charming. And the idea of setting a Shakespearean tragedy in the Caribbean— what country was that?

HOUSEMAN
Haiti.

COUNTESS
Haiti. Carlo commented to me afterward that he hadn't seen anything like it and he's from Vienna, you know.

CARLO
Si, multi bello. Velikey Bolshoy.

COUNTESS
Carlo is an extraordinarily talented composer, Jack. I would be very interested in cultivating a relationship between yourself, Mr. Welles, and Carlo. What is the name of your opera, dear?

CARLO
Le Cordonier Désespère.

The Haitian Play

In the film *Cradle Will Rock*, the fictional Countess La Grange (Vanessa Redgrave) informs her steel-mogul husband over breakfast that it is bad luck—potentially even fatal—to say "Macbeth" inside a theatre. Instead, actors call Shakespeare's harrowing drama of murderous ambition the "Scottish play." The Countess, like many real-life theatregoers, was swept off her feet by a revolutionary production of the "Scottish play" transplanted to Haiti and pushed to bold extremes by an "all-Negro" cast directed by a twenty-year-old wunderkind named Orson Welles.

Welles's role in the production that became known as the "voodoo" *Macbeth* is a tale of high drama in and of itself. Soon after the FTP was formed in 1935, Rose McClendon, the head of New York's Negro unit and a veteran African-American actress, requested that John Houseman be appointed as her codirector. Hallie Flanagan noted that McClendon "felt that since Negroes had always been performers and had no previous means of learning direction, they would prefer to start under more experienced direction." The well-connected Houseman, in turn, hired Welles. Though it wasn't the FTP's most seasoned leadership, no one could have surpassed the Welles-Houseman team for energy and flamboyance.

As a result, the interpersonal pyrotechnics on the set matched the intensity of those performed beneath the proscenium. During rehearsals the emotional pitch ran so high that the production's star, Jack Carter—who went on to act in *Faustus* and *The Cradle Will Rock*—threatened to walk out. One man, convinced that Welles was trying to humiliate blacks, attacked him with a razor. Even Flanagan admitted that the actors were often "threatening to murder Orson in spite of their admiration for him." But in the end, it was this admiration, fueled by Welles's contagious belief that the company was making historic theatre, that focused the actors' talents and crystallized their success.

Opening night drew Broadway regulars uptown and brought Harlem residents onto the street in droves. Behind police barricades, a crowd of ten thousand spectators milled around the Lafayette Theatre, eager for a glimpse of what was brewing inside, and scalpers had no trouble pocketing $3 for tickets marked 40¢.

Behind the curtain, the Lafayette's stage had been transformed into nineteenth-century Haiti of the mind. Bathed in Abe Feder's eerie spotlights, the battlements of designer Nat Karson's fantastic castle reared over the treetops of his lush "Caribbean" jungle. As the shrieking of witches gave way to the opening strains of Virgil Thomson's score—powerfully augmented by the drums of an Ethiopian percussion ensemble—the audience knew it was in the grip of an irresistible theatrical spell.

For ten weeks voodoo *Macbeth* played to sold-out houses in New York, before embarking on a national tour. *New York Times* critic Brooks Atkinson called the production "a triumph of theatre art." But there were also notable pans, including the one offered by Percy Hammond, an anti–New Deal critic who pronounced the show "an exhibition of deluxe boondoggling" and expressed outrage that Welles's shenanigans were being funded out of the public till. When Hammond was found dead a few days later, the coroner called it a heart attack. But the actors had a better story: the "voodoo" had gotten to him.

A scene from the Lafayette Theatre's all-black production of Macbeth.

COUNTESS

Cobbler in Despair. He sings me passages from it all the time. He can't seem to get it out of his head, poor Carlo. Such a sad man.

Carlo doesn't seem sad.

HOUSEMAN

Ssssh.

INT. MAXINE ELLIOTT'S THEATRE. DAY.

Houseman opens the door to the theatre with the Countess and Carlo, taking seats in the back. Doctor Faustus is in rehearsal. Mephistopheles (Canada Lee) in a beam of light.

MEPHISTOPHELES (CANADA LEE)

Now his heart blood dries with grief.
His conscience kills it, and his labouring brain
Begets a world of idle fantasies
To overreach the devil. But all in vain.
His store of pleasures must be sauced with pain.

Mephistopheles disappears, leaving Faustus (Welles) screaming. In an instant, six scholars appear.

1ST SCHOLAR (SILVANO)

Now, worthy Faustus, methinks your looks are changed.

FAUSTUS (WELLES)

Oh gentlemen!

5TH SCHOLAR (ADAIR)

What ails Faustus?

FAUSTUS (WELLES)

Look, sirs, comes he not? Comes he not? *(as himself)* That is the cymbal crash. Pick up the cues.

1ST SCHOLAR (SILVANO)

Be like he is grown into some sickness by being over solitary. It's but a surfeit. Never fear, man.

FAUSTUS (WELLES)

A surfeit of deadly sin. Cue lightning.

2ND SCHOLAR (GEER)

Yet, Faustus, look up to heaven.

A beat; then lightning strikes.

WELLES

That was late. When the cue is late it will get a laugh. We don't need this laugh. It is a stupid, embarrassing laugh. Concentrate, folks. *(as Faustus)* But Faustus' offenses can never be pardoned: the serpent that tempted Eve may be saved, but not Faustus . . .

4TH SCHOLAR (HIRAM)

Yet, Faustus, call on God.

FAUSTUS (WELLES)

On God whom Faustus hath abjured! Ah, my God, I would weep, but the Devil draws in my tears. I would lift up my hands, but see, they hold them, they hold them!

4TH SCHOLAR (HIRAM)

Who, Faustus?

FAUSTUS (WELLES)

Lucifer and Mephistopheles. Ah, gentlemen, I gave them my soul for my cunning.

Canada Lee appears in a flash of light.

MARVEL

Cue?

DULCE

Not your line.

MARVEL

What's my line?

DULCE

Not yours. It's Bert's. Bert, say your line.

3RD SCHOLAR (BERT)

It's his. Oh God forbid!

MARVEL

Oh God forbid!

FAUSTUS (WELLES)

God forbade it indeed . . .

Most baby boomers remember Norman Lloyd for his role as the wise and avuncular Dr. Daniel Auschlander on the popular eighties' TV drama *St. Elsewhere*. But he's also had a long career in film acting—with appearances in *The Age of Innocence, Dead Poet's Society,* Hitchcock's *Sabateur,* and Jean Renoir's *The Southerners*—as well as in producing and directing for television. Recent projects include roles in Universal's live action–animation mix *Rocky and Bullwinkle* and in the PBS film of Willa Cather's *Song of the Lark.*

Though in his mid-eighties today, Lloyd remembers clearly his days working for the Federal Theatre Project more than sixty years ago. It was director Joseph Losey who brought him in, having seen him perform in a play in Boston, offering him the standard weekly relief salary of $23.87. When Losey gave him the script for the Living Newspaper *Injunction Granted,* Lloyd initially saw no role for himself. Later that same week, however, he went to see Barnum & Bailey's circus under a tent on Nostrand Avenue in Brooklyn and realized what the play needed: a clown. With Losey's blessing, Lloyd originated the role.

Lloyd appeared in a total of three Living Newspaper productions: *Triple-A Plowed Under, Injunction Granted,* and *Power.* "My best notice ever," says the actor, "was in a newletter published by Con Edison [the electric and gas utility] trying to discredit *Power.* They took particular note of 'a very clever actor playing a consumer.' That was me—Angus J. Buttonkooper."

Lloyd went on to work for the short-lived Mercury Theatre, appearing in the Welles-Houseman version of *Julius Caesar.* Marc Blitzstein himself, with whom he had worked in *I've Got the Tune,* asked him to be in Mercury's production of *The Cradle Will Rock,* but Lloyd turned him down. "I didn't want another flashy small part," he says of his thinking at the time. It was a decision he has always regretted.

After Mercury broke up, Lloyd rejoined the FTP briefly for *Sing for Your Supper.* While in rehearsal, he received a $200-a-week offer from Max Gordon and George S. Kaufman to be in Harold Rome's *Sing Out the News,* but turned them down because he had "promised Hallie." His loyalty would cost him. Soon afterward, Max

> **❝I want this play and plays like it done from one end of the country to the other. . . . People will say it's propaganda. Well, I say what of it? The big power companies have spent millions on propaganda for the utilities. It's about time the consumer had a mouthpiece.❞**
>
> —Harry Hopkins, backstage to the cast of *Power*

Gordon ran into WPA director Harry Hopkins at the racetrack in Laurel, Maryland.

MG: You must have a great thing going on.

HH: What do you mean?

MG: I offered Norman Lloyd a part in a great musical and he turned me down—what have you got going there?

HH: Tax, tax, spend, spend, elect, elect—that's how we do it.

Despite the humor he displayed, Hopkins subsequently ordered Lloyd fired—it was illegal for an actor to pass up market-rate work in favor of relief work.

Yet Lloyd remained a staunch supporter of the FTP and in particular the woman at its helm. "She was iron," he said of Flanagan, but the administration "would only go so far." They censored *Ethiopia,* and when it came to *Cradle,* he says, "somebody got to her."

He also feels lucky to have worked with the dynamic Houseman and Welles. "John Houseman was a glory for the theatre. A doer. He animated people and productions wherever he went." In the late 1940s, Lloyd and Houseman ran the Coronet Theatre in Los Angeles, where the Bertolt Brecht play *Galileo,* produced by T. Edward Hambleton and directed by Joe Losey, had its world premier.

"But Orson Welles could stage a scene like no one else. He was the first American director to create totality in his productions—an integration of play, sound, lighting—the 'event' quality. It had been done in Europe, but never in the U.S. Before Orson, we had great directors, but they were super-stage managers by comparison. In a Welles production the audience was surrounded by the vastness of ideas and execution.

"You see, we were politically aware. Under the WPA everything was pulsing—creating, creating, creating. Even in New York, many people had never seen live theatre. Our cap price was only 85 cents, and people would really respond. In *Triple-A Plowed Under,* they cheered the John L. Lewis character and booed the Earl Browder character [the Communist Party Chairman]. We had to convince them it was only a play! The audience was moved by theatre, it saw itself up there. I remember sitting on stage during that play and thinking: 'This is glorious.'"

Above: Norman Lloyd, here applying clown makeup for his role in Injunction Granted. *Left:* Power, *a Living Newspaper that called for public ownership of utilities, opened in New York in February 1937. In this scene Lloyd appears on the left.*

ADAIR

Break time.

FAUSTUS (WELLES)

. . . but Faustus hath done it . . .

ADAIR

Break time, union break, fifteen minutes.

WELLES

I writ them a bill with mine own blood: the date is expired, the hell with theatre, the hell with you, I've got to go have a coffee and a fart. Never mind that for the first time in this goddamn rehearsal process we were in the middle of a discovery essential to making this play work! I NEED A SMOKE. Go on get out go have a fucking day-long smoke—you can all fuck off. You aren't actors, you are smokers. You wouldn't know the church of the theatre if it smacked you in the mouth.

ADAIR

Shut up, Orson, or I'll smack you in the mouth.

WELLES

Fuck you, John. You aren't a believer. You're a worker.

ADAIR

Damn right. And you're not a director. You're a dictator, Orson.

WELLES

You are atheists; worse yet, you are the mildly faithful, coin in hand to chuck into the collection plate without a true belief in you, lusting after the end of the ceremony. You have absolutely no respect for theatre, for the process. This isn't a game, this isn't a goddamn cocktail party; it's work, hard work, and if you aren't willing to dedicate your blood to it, it is not worth it. You will never make theatre with these coffee klatch union breaks; you will make pageants, without truth, without soul, bloodless, sweatless, shallow lily-white pageants signifying nothing!

Throughout the previous dialogue, Welles has left the stage and gone into the house of the theatre. He now sees Houseman, the Countess, and Carlo.

WELLES

I'm going, Jack. Give them a two-hour smoke. We'll pick up with the seven deadly sins.

Welles leaves the theatre.

HOUSEMAN

He has his moments.

CARLO

He is busto, multidissimo.

COUNTESS

Fascinating. I've always wanted to observe the process of art-making. What happens now?

HOUSEMAN

Now we wait for the prima donna to return.

Bill Murray as the cranky ventriloquist Tommy Crickshaw. Crickshaw's character was based loosely on the real-life Frank Merlin, whom Flanagan picked to head the FTP vaudeville unit. "Is it a hard job and does it pay anything?" was all Merlin wanted to know before accepting the position.

VOICE

Sandra.

We see Sandra Mescal come up the aisle.

SANDRA

Baby!

The voice belongs to Will Geer, who runs to Sandra and she to him. They embrace right next to where the Countess is and fall to the floor making wild passionate love.

HOUSEMAN (*to Countess*)

They're in love, you see.

Silvano approaches Houseman.

SILVANO

Excuse me, Mr. Houseman, but I have to go to the hospital.

HOUSEMAN

The hospital, why? Are you hurt?

SILVANO

No. (*To Countess*) Hello. I . . .

COUNTESS

How do you do?

SILVANO

Hi. (*To Houseman*) My wife just had a child.

HOUSEMAN

Congratulations.

SILVANO

Thank you.

HOUSEMAN

Countess, may I introduce a supporting member of our cast, Aldo Silvano. He plays the role of the um . . .

SILVANO

Fourth Scholar.

COUNTESS

Wonderful.

INT. VAUDEVILLE THEATRE DRESSING ROOM. DAY.

The ventriloquist, Crickshaw, alone backstage, speaks to the mirror. His dummy lays lifeless on a table nearby. A "Dissatisfied with Federal Theatre?" flyer is on his mirror.

CRICKSHAW

This ain't no political meeting house, it's a damn theatre. We're not doin' nothing but entertaining, making people laugh.

Crickshaw's vaudeville trainees Larry and Sid, played by Kyle Gass and Jack Black.

DUMMY

Well, I'm making people laugh. Get me up.

CRICKSHAW

Mrs. Flanagan wants me to teach these Reds how to make people laugh.

DUMMY

Ha! Forget it. You?

CRICKSHAW

There's nothing funny about Communists.

DUMMY

There's nothing funny about you.

CRICKSHAW

Reds are glum, serious people.

DUMMY

What about that Stinky Magoo? He was funny.

CRICKSHAW

He wasn't a Communist.

DUMMY

Most certainly was. As Red as a rooster's crown.

CRICKSHAW

Melvin, you don't know what you're talking about. Stinky Magoo was a Republican.

DUMMY

He was Red, Tommy. I know.

CRICKSHAW

He wasn't a Red. Stinky Magoo was a Republican and he was funny.

Bolshevik Beavers & Would-Be Boys

So highly charged was the atmosphere surrounding the Federal Theatre Project that its "free, adult" productions often could not help but tread on a broad spectrum of tender political toes. Nor could they completely evade censorship. One Living Newspaper, *Ethiopia*—openly critical of Mussolini and Fascism—ran afoul of FDR's appeasement policies and was abruptly closed down on orders from the Oval Office.

But in 1937, as now, the media's influence on children raised partisan sentiment to its highest pitch. It is not surprising, then, that it was a children's play, *Revolt of the Beavers*, by Oscar Saul and Lou Lanz, that drew the most furious accusations of "Communistic" content in a flap that quickly assumed surrealistic proportions.

Revolt of the Beavers was a madcap fable for the times that carried a distinctly subversive edge. Even Hallie Flanagan admitted that this tale of furry, buck-toothed mammals conspiring to overthrow a ruthless beaver overlord and set up a new order where all things are equally shared was "very class conscious." It was also hilariously funny and brilliantly staged, featuring a roller-skating cast and a barber's chair sitting in for the "King of the Beavers" throne. Plus, it actively encouraged audience participation.

The play proved wildly popular with young audiences, but entirely unsettling to many guardians of their future citizenship—even those nominally in support of the FTP. In his *New York Times* review, Brooks Atkinson fulminated that "many children unschooled in the technique of revolution now have an opportunity, at government expense, to improve their tender minds. Mother Goose is no longer a rhymed escapist. She has been studying Marx; Jack and Jill lead the class revolution."

Flanagan tried to defend the show, but *Beavers* proved so controversial that the FTP

was forced to pull the plug after only a month, even as it continued to draw enthusiastic audiences.

An equally energetic FTP children's production that lacked *Beavers*'s political liabilities was Yasha Frank's staging of *Pinocchio*—the nineteenth-century tale of a wooden puppet who wants to become a real boy. Featuring dialogue in verse and an original musical score, *Pinocchio* ran for over a year in Los Angeles, fueled by audiences—as high as 75 percent adult—that were often returning to see it for the sixth or seventh time.

One of the secrets of *Pinocchio*'s enduring success was that Frank's version had upped the fable's hilarity and underplayed its grimmer aspects. But the night the curtain fell on FTP projects across the country, Frank and his cast improvised an ending that turned Pinocchio's final performance into a parable of outrage over the fate of the national theatre. As Flanagan describes it in her biography, *Arena*, "Pinocchio, having conquered selfishness and greed, did not become a living boy. Instead he was turned back into a puppet. 'So let the bells proclaim our grief,' intoned the company at the finish, 'that his small life was all too brief.'" With the audience watching, the stagehands demolished the set, and placed Pinocchio in a coffin inscribed with the epitaph: *Killed by Act of Congress, June 30, 1939.*

Unlike the rest of the FTP, however, *Pinocchio* lived on. A still-young Walt Disney, along with his technical staff, had attended eight performances of the play in Los Angeles. A year later, Disney released his own cartoon version of the classic tale.

> **❝In it there are sequences which approach more closely the classic works of Walt Disney than anything I have seen the stage produce. There is a beautiful undersea fantasy; there is a charming marionette sequence; there is, in fact, that kind of simple, imaginative fancy running through the production that not only delights a child's heart but touches responsive chords in the minds of the older and ostensibly wiser generation.❞**
>
> —Robert Rice's review of *Pinocchio* in the *New York Telegraph*, 1939

Left: Yasha Frank's stage version of Pinocchio, *first performed in Los Angeles in 1937, was an immediate hit. Top right: Revolt of the Beavers, a children's play by Oscar Saul and Lou Lanz, seemed to confirm the suspicions of FTP critics that the children's unit was a hotbed of radical activity.*

DUMMY
He was funny, you are right about that.

CRICKSHAW
God rest his soul.

DUMMY
May he make God laugh.

CRICKSHAW
Here, here.

Crickshaw takes a drink. There's a knock on the door.

SID
Mr. Crickshaw. We're ready for our tutorial.

Sid and Larry are there.

LARRY
We're ready for our tutorial.

SID
We're ready to learn how to be funny.

LARRY
And how to do the mouth thing.

INT. MUSEUM. DAY.

A private reception preview of the Italian Art Exhibit for large donors and press. Champagne and caviar circulate on palate trays held by waiters in art smocks. Margherita Sarfatti, a well-dressed, powerful Italian woman in her forties, walks with Gray Mathers, William Randolph Hearst, and Marion Davies. Sarfatti, Mathers, and Hearst are looking at a Futurist painting. Press hover about.

Margherita Sarfatti (Susan Sarandon) pours over priceless artworks with American corporate moguls William Randolph Hearst (John Carpenter) and the young Nelson Rockefeller (John Cusack), above right.

SARFATTI
It is an art form that embraces the future, that shatters convention, uses color to create an exquisite sensuality.

MATHERS
It looks all cut up. Shapes distributed geometrically.

SARFATTI
Exactly. Very perceptive.

HEARST
What does it mean?

SARFATTI
It can mean whatever you want it to mean. The Futurists exist in the realm of emotion, the Eros, not the intellect.

MATHERS
Yes, Eros. I particularly like the sensuality of the colors.

SARFATTI
You have a very good eye, Mr. Mathers.

MATHERS
Gray.

SARFATTI
Gray?

MATHERS
My name, not the color.

Nelson Rockefeller, dashing, rich, and twenty-six years old, approaches.

ROCKEFELLER
Is that a Modigliani?

SARFATTI
Why, yes it is.

MATHERS
Nelson Rockefeller, meet Margherita Sarfatti, cultural emissary to president Mussolini. Delighted to see you, Nelson.

ROCKEFELLER
Mr. Mathers, Mr. Hearst. Always a pleasure. Good to see you Marion.

SARFATTI
The Italian Government is very thankful to you and your family for your generous contribution to the museum. From what I understand you have been instrumental in bringing this exhibition here.

26

ROCKEFELLER

My motives are purely selfish, Madame. I have never in my life been lucky enough to stand inches away from a Da Vinci or a Michelangelo.

SARFATTI

How does it feel?

ROCKEFELLER

Extraordinary.

HEARST

Nelson can be very helpful in the oil department as well, my dear.

SARFATTI

Really?

HEARST

Oh, there I go again jumping the gun, ruining a perfectly civil conversation on art by getting to the point.

Mathers laughs loudly.

ROCKEFELLER

I must confess I am more interested in the oil in paint than the oil in derricks.

Laughter.

ROCKEFELLER

I understand you know Diego Rivera.

SARFATTI

Yes, Paris. Wild times.

ROCKEFELLER

I'm to see him today. Any tips?

SARFATTI

Swing left. Stay sober. He was once a cannibal, you know.

EXT. UNION SQUARE. DAY.

An agitated Marc Blitzstein walks through a crowd of laborers and protesters and we follow him. We are at a workers' rally. Banners of vivid colors. Chanting from many sources. A crowd has gathered to hear a speech. On a box stands a union leader. We stay primarily on Blitzstein as he watches; at times his thoughts are heard, at times lines from songs in The Cradle Will Rock. *A writer's perceptions are what carry this scene, not the politics of the speaker.*

JASPER (V.O.)

Five dead, two shot in the back, twenty-seven injured by the blackjacks and fists of the strike breakers. And who were the attackers, the murderers? Ladies and gentlemen, the murderers last night were government employees. Policemen

killing and beating the very citizens who pay their wages, lending their nightsticks and guns to the industrialists to the strike breakers.

The camera reaches a bench where Blitzstein sits. Bertolt Brecht appears next to him.

BRECHT

What is your play about?

BLITZSTEIN

A prostitute.

BRECHT

That's survival, that's not enough. What about the other prostitutes? You don't have to be poor to be a whore. Look around you. In the mansions, in the churches, in the universities. Everyone is corruptible, even your union leaders.

INT. VAUDEVILLE THEATRE. DAY.

Crickshaw stands on stage in an empty theatre. Two apprentice entertainers, Sid and Larry, are by his side. Crickshaw stands with dummy, Sid and Larry with their hands up pretending to move the mouths of their imaginary dummies.

SID

Now who's the dummy?

LARRY

Now who's the dummy?

CRICKSHAW

You want to move the back of the mouth. Try it again.

SID

Now who's the dummy?

Although the *Detroit News*

reported in 1937 that "the sit-down has replaced base-ball as a national pastime," Americans still found time for plenty of less risky activities. Movie palaces across the nation transported Depression-weary audiences to a host of exotic locales, among them rural China in the screen adaptation of Pearl S. Buck's *The Good Earth* and Shangri-La in Frank Capra's *Lost Horizon*. Topper's Cary Grant and Constance Bennett proved that being a ghost was no impediment to living the good life in a Manhattan penthouse. And however inscrutable the mysteries of the economy, moviegoers could always count on Charlie Chan nabbing his man by the end of the second reel.

For radio listeners tuned into *Our Gal Sunday*, the burning question was "Can a girl from a mining town in the West find happiness as the wife of a wealthy and titled Englishman?" And, although no one can say for certain if Hazel Huffman (Joan Cusack) heard the sexy repartee between Mae West and ventriloquist Edgar Bergen's sidekick Charlie McCarthy, she would no doubt have been scandalized. West's lascivious appraisal of the wise-cracking dummy, "Ooh, I can see you're all wood and a yard long," provoked a storm of protest and an FCC crackdown on off-color, on-air humor.

While the stock market dived to a new four-year low, the surging popularity of jazz was winning millions of fresh adherents to the catchy, sophisticated, and uniquely African-American musical form long derided by snobs and bigots as "jungle music." Whether lindy-ing to Fats Waller's "The Joint Is Jumpin'" or Benny Goodman's "Sing, Sing, Sing," young Americans were bridging class and racial chasms on the dance floor.

In literature, Margaret Mitchell's *Gone with the Wind*,

Zora Neale Hurston's *Their Eyes Were Watching God*, and John Steinbeck's *Of Mice and Men* all vied for readership in 1937. The year's runaway best-seller, Dale and Dorothy Carnegie's *How to Win Friends and Influence People*, single-handedly launched a new and enduring industry in self-improvement, while beyond the spotlight, Ezra Pound's *Cantos* raged in dark poetic cadences that would soon turn explicitly Fascist.

A wave of industrial and scientific innovations—harbingers of post–World War II suburban consumer culture—was unveiled. From locomotives to pencil sharpeners, the promise of a streamlined, effortless future was transforming the look and feel of everyday life. The year 1937 saw the first household refrigerators roll off assembly lines, ready to be plugged into the WPA's advancing hydroelectric grid. Soon owners of prefabricated homes could drive their automatic transmission GM cars to A & P's prototype supermarkets, where they would find shelves stocked with Hormel's canned Spam and General Mills's corn-puffed Kix.

But advertisers, aware that mass-market products aimed at the prosperous future were still a tough sell, often kept their tongues planted firmly in cheek. One popular commercial featured a bankrupt young couple trying to outdo one another at self-sacrifice. "Where's your gold bridgework?" Annie asks her husband, only to find he has traded it for an armload of Niblets Brand Corn. "Oh Henry, you darling, but I hocked the gas range to get you these Green Giant Brand Peas." What a dilemma! Fortunately, "Niblets are good enough to eat without cooking, and Green Giants are tender enough to eat without teeth!"

Above: Union chefs at the Willard Hotel in Washington, D.C., sit down on a cold stove in protest, 1937. Left: Jozie De Simone and Mimie Gnazzo dancing the lindy hop, named after Charles Lindbergh, in 1940 at the Daily News Harvest Moon Ball at Roseland. Right: The year 1938 saw the introduction of Superman, courtesy of Action Comics. While their parents read the first issues of Newsweek, kids found their own diversion in the adventures of cartoon heroes and villains.

Sit Down & Swing

LARRY

Now who's the dummy?

Mo and Larry are terrible ventriloquists.

CRICKSHAW

Your mouth is moving. If your mouth is moving the effect is ruined. Try to keep your lips immobile.

Mo and Larry try, grinning and laughing at themselves. These Commies aren't funny.

INT. FEDERAL THEATRE OFFICES/HALLIE'S OFFICE. DAY.

HALLIE

"Federal Theatre's touring show 'Broadway Bandwagon' rolled into Peoria last night and for two hours gaiety and glamour obscured thoughts of drought and other financial worries." *Peoria Star*. They performed in Dubuque, Waterloo, Eau Claire, Sheboygan, Wausau, Wisconsin Rapids. I saw it at a high school in Manitowoc. Three thousand students seeing their first play with live actors. It was very exciting.

DE ROHAN

I just got a letter from Portland Oregon's director. Their debut is a resounding success. Sold out shows every night.

O'HARA

Denver is a week away from opening *Rake's Progress*. That will be Colorado's debut.

HALLIE

It Can't Happen Here?

DE ROHAN

It Can't Happen Here is a steamroller. We've got a commitment from the Detroit project.

O'HARA

Also the Seattle Negro Company is in.

ROSE

And Brooklyn is doing a version in Yiddish.

O'HARA

Twenty-four productions in seventeen states, all opening on the same day.

HALLIE

Fantastic.

DE ROHAN

A national theatre, Hallie.

O'HARA

. . . Newark, Bridgeport, Yonkers, Staten Island, Tampa . . .

Music is playing in the next room. Rose has exited. Hallie follows. We move to see the Beaverman and Beaverwoman singing.

INT. HOSPITAL MATERNITY WARD. DAY.

Amongst a long row of beds with other new mothers is Sophie Silvano. Aldo sits goo-gooing with their newborn baby.

SOPHIE

Did he stomp his feet?

SILVANO

A couple times.

SOPHIE

He sounds like such a child.

SILVANO

Let's not talk about Orson. Let's talk about Antonio.

SOPHIE

Antonio?

SILVANO

You don't like it?

SOPHIE

I like it.

SILVANO

He's beautiful. You made this. You're amazing. You're the artist.

SOPHIE

Thank you. I take pride in my work.

We hear a voice.

VOICE

Dov'è il mio nuovo nipote?

SOPHIE

Your mother.

SILVANO

There's only one voice like it.

MAMA

I thought I'd find you in a room.

SILVANO

This is a room.

MAMA

A big room, yes. I thought I'd find you without so many people.

Aldo Silvano (John Turturro); his wife, Sophie (Barbara Sukowa); and his mother (Lynn Cohen) coo over the couple's newborn son.

SILVANO

We couldn't afford that.

MAMA

Poverino, if your papa had a better job you could get a better room.

SILVANO

I don't want to start this, Mama. Speak good things in front of my son.

MAMA

There's so many people. Someone could be sick.

SILVANO

Say hello to Sophie.

MAMA

Hello, Sophie.

SOPHIE

Hello, Mama.

MAMA

Look at that face.

INT. MUSEUM. DAY.

Countess, Carlo, and Mathers.

COUNTESS

Today I saw Mr. Welles throw a tantrum in front of his new cast. They are mostly white. He was so passionate.

MATHERS

I'm sure. You're late, you know.

COUNTESS

Have I missed much? Have any of the paintings moved?

MATHERS

Most of the people have.

COUNTESS

Look, a Da Vinci. Splendid.

Pause.

COUNTESS

Sublime, really.

Pause.

MATHERS

Hearst says the Federal Theatre is full of Reds.

COUNTESS

Communists?

CARLO

Communists?

COUNTESS

I can't imagine that to be true.

MATHERS

Hearst is a smart man.

COUNTESS

Yes, and I suppose I am a dim woman.

MATHERS

I didn't say that.

COUNTESS

Perhaps Mr. Hearst could explain to me the Communist implications of The Scottish Play in the Caribbean?

They approach Sarfatti and Hearst.

MATHERS

Margherita Sarfatti. My wife, the perpetually late Countess La Grange.

COUNTESS

Charmed.

SARFATTI

Likewise. Your husband has an excellent eye for art. You are a lucky woman to have such a cultured man.

COUNTESS

I'm blessed really.

HEARST

Margherita, we must go.

MATHERS

Miss Sarfatti, it has been a pleasure talking to you. You can assure your trade representative that Mathers Steel will put frames on Italian trucks as long as wheels turn.

SARFATTI

I am sure it will be deeply appreciated.

MATHERS

Anything we can do to stop the spread of Communism in Europe is in our own best interest.

SARFATTI

Thank you. Good day, sir.

She exits.

COUNTESS

Did you just make a business deal?

MATHERS

No, dear.

COUNTESS
You just said you'd put frames on Italian trucks.

MATHERS
That's none of your business, dear.

INT. VAUDEVILLE THEATRE. DAY.
Sid and Larry continue their tutorial.

LARRY
Mr. Darwin claims that it took a hundred thousand years for a man to make a monk . . . for a monk . . . for a man . . . For nature to make a monkey out of a man.

SID
That's nothing. A man can make . . . a woman can make a monkey out of a man in an hour.

LARRY
That's true.

SID
Like your wife made a monkey out of you.

LARRY
Melvin, people don't have to know that.

Crickshaw's training sessions with Sid and Larry are not going well.

CRICKSHAW
All right. Those are my jokes you're butchering, my act. I know you two probably don't believe in personal property, but this is not Russia, this is not rice or grain. This is my property, my act. You do not do another entertainer's act. It is not done. Understood?

SID
O.K. Yes, sir.

LARRY
Yes, sir.

SID
Now who's the dummy?

INT. HOSPITAL MATERNITY WARD. DAY.
The family has grown. The men have cigars in their mouths. Brothers, nephews, aunts mill about.

UNCLE
I saw in the paper that that Welles you work with is the voice of the Shadow.

MAMA
I like that show.

PAPA
Marta learns English from that show.

MARTA
The Shadow knows.

UNCLE
So he's famous.

SILVANO
He works a lot.

UNCLE
He's got money, right?

SILVANO
Yes.

UNCLE
So why can't you do that?

SILVANO
I'd like to.

UNCLE
So what's stopping you?

SILVANO
You've got to get the job.

UNCLE
So apply for it. Wait on line for it.

SILVANO
It doesn't work that way.

UNCLE
You're lazy. You gotta get up early, wait on line.

MARTA
Early bird cassus warm.

SILVANO
You don't wait on line for a theatre job. You audition, you try out, you read. You pretend to be the character; you don't wait on line.

UNCLE
I'm smackin' this guy.

SILVANO
I've got to pick the kids up at school.

SOPHIE
They're going to Vincent's.

SILVANO
I'm taking them to rehearsal.

He takes the baby and gives him to Sophie. Sophie takes the child to her breast.

SILVANO
I love you, my artist.

He kisses Sophie on the forehead and leaves.

EXT. UNION SQUARE. DAY.
Blitzstein composing at a piano. From another angle we see that Blitzstein is imagining fingerings, working out a tune in his head. A woman's voice joins his as they sing "Joe Worker." A line of policemen is approaching, clubs in hand.

LISTEN, HERE'S A STORY,
NOT MUCH FUN AND NOT MUCH GLORY.
LOW CLASS, LOWDOWN,
THE THING YOU NEVER CARE TO SEE
UNTIL THERE IS A SHOWDOWN.

The speaker continues his speech. A line of policemen approach. Shoving, pushing, provocation. A riot. Blitzstein voice recedes. The woman sings.

HOW MANY FAKERS,
PEACE UNDERTAKERS, PAID STRIKE BREAKERS,
HOW MANY TOILING, AILING, DYING
PILED-UP BODIES, BROTHER,
DOES IT TAKE TO MAKE YOU WISE?

The riot continues. Brecht and Eva stand behind Blitzstein.

BRECHT
It's very serious.

EVA
Where's the irony? Where's the humor?

BRECHT
What about the other prostitutes?

Blitzstein stands on a bench and berates the police. A mounted policeman approaches, club at the ready.

EXT. RIVERA APARTMENT. DAY.
Nelson Rockefeller looks at address and down to his hand.

INT. RIVERA APARTMENT. DAY.
Rockefeller enters.

ROCKEFELLER
Hello. Mr. Rivera? Diego Rivera?

Rivera comes from the back.

DIEGO RIVERA
Sí.

ROCKEFELLER
I'm Nelson Rockefeller. I send greetings from Margherita Sarfatti. She says she knows you.

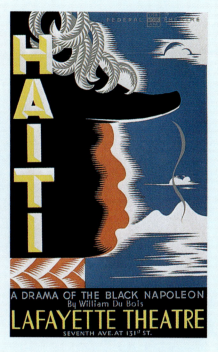

Some of the posters created for FTP productions by artists supported under the WPA's Federal Art Project.

Today, everything from cars to peanut butter to what's playing at the local cineplex is advertised on TV. But in 1937, posters were the dominant venue of advertising, so if you wanted to keep up with the times, you had to read the walls. Vying for attention with ads for Moxie and Marlboro (then being promoted as a classy "women's cigarette") were bold posters for FTP productions of *Faustus, Pinocchio,* and *Big White Fog,* among others. These highly graphic artworks, as well as others that urged Americans to "STOP the Spread of Syphilis," "Work with Care," "Report Dog Bites," and later, as the country entered World War II, "Salvage Scrap to Blast the Jap," emerged from the drawing boards of artists funded by the WPA's Federal Art Project (FAP).

The idea for the FAP came from George Biddle, a blueblood Philadelphia artist and former classmate of FDR, who had studied with the great Mexican muralists Diego Rivera and José Clemente Orozco. Biddle, who became director of the agency, built community art centers throughout the South and West, where hundreds of murals—whose primary subject matter was America at work—were created. The FAP's six thousand artists also produced thousands of sculptures, oil paintings, watercolors, prints, and graphic designs, and an astonishing quarter of a million photographs that brought the immensity of the Depression down to the scale of a human face.

Though the style employed by most of the FAP poster artists was populist and representational, the strong geometrics of their compositions and saturated colors both influenced and dovetailed with the emerging abstractionism of members of the FAP "easel painter" unit, among them Jackson Pollock, Ad Reinhardt, and Willem de Kooning. And women came closer to aesthetic parity than at any time before or since: nationwide, fully 41 percent of WPA artists, including painter Alice Neel, sculptor Louise Nevelson, and photographers Dorothea Lange, Margaret Bourke-White, and Berenice Abbott, were female.

The FAP also acted as a "cradle" for technical innovation. Anthony Velonis of New York City's poster division adapted commercial silkscreening to a fine-arts process (serigraphy) that allowed for the production of eight-color, hand-pulled posters at the rate of six hundred per day. Velonis's technique was later given further cachet and taken to new levels of sophistication by Pop artists Andy Warhol, Roy Lichtenstein, and Robert Rauschenberg.

Few of the FAP's poster artists—whose number included Richard Floethe, Veer Block, and Velonis (who designed the poster for voodoo *Macbeth*)—went on to achieve the fame of their contemporaries in the "easel painting" division. Most of the creators of the surviving two thousand WPA posters, of the estimated 2 million originally produced, remain unknown. Nor was their work, labeled "boondoggle art" by contemporary conservatives, universally appreciated. But art historian Francis V. O'Connor, who discovered a forgotten cache in a corner tower of the Library of Congress, saw in these "murals in miniature" evidence that "something revolutionary happened to American culture during the 1930s."

Poster Children

Big White Fog

Voodoo Macbeth scored an early, unequivocal victory for the Federal Theatre Project, and in particular its Negro unit. It also set a benchmark for Flanagan's goal of making innovative theatre that aroused real-world passions. But in pursuing its mission, the FTP offended the racial attitudes of many white Americans at the time, represented in Robbins's film by the puritanical Hazel Huffman. As the movie suggests, it was sexual paranoia about "race mixing," even more than virulent anti-Communism, that eventually brought down the FTP.

From our perspective today, it is difficult to imagine a theatre as segregated in the early 1930s as any other aspect of American life—from baseball to the armed forces. Added to this, the economic woes of the Depression spelled double jeopardy for black Americans who now found themselves disproportionately unemployed and even more sharply discriminated against. Three years before the triumphant voodoo *Macbeth*, lynchings in this country surged to a high of twenty-four.

In 1931, nine black men known collectively as the "Scottsboro Boys" were falsely convicted of rape in Alabama, and eight of them sentenced to death. Though the capital sentences were eventually overturned, five of the defendants served long prison sentences for a crime that, it was later acknowledged, had never occurred.

Even the New Deal agencies were not immune to insidious racism. Since he owed much of his power to southern Democrats, Roosevelt never made black equality part of his agenda. In fact, the Agricultural Adjustment Act accelerated the displacement of black sharecroppers

to the point where it was cynically referred to as the "Negro Removal Act"—a play on the initials of the New Deal's National Recovery Administration. And relief programs routinely reinforced segregation in housing and the workplace. "You can raise all the rumpus you like," said one official. "We just aren't going to mix Negroes and white folks in any village in TVA."

Given this context, the Federal Theatre must have seemed a truly progressive—or threatening, depending on where you stood—force. Segregation there was far less rigid than in the vast majority of contemporary theatre, where black actors could not play leading roles in white productions, physical contact between black men and white women was strictly forbidden, and many white actors refused to appear onstage with blacks. Though the FTP maintained racially and ethnically divided companies, in Boston the black unit shared a building with Yiddish and other FTP drama groups, and presented plays with mixed casts.

Overall, the FTP sponsored sixteen Negro units with a total of 851 members. Besides the voodoo *Macbeth*, New York's Lafayette unit alone mounted twenty-nine shows between 1935 and 1939. Black companies produced a wide variety of drama, including classics like *Lysistrata* and *The Mikado*, in addition to works by Shaw and O'Neill.

But one of the most significant legacies of the FTP lay in its production of works by contemporary African-American dramatists. Theodore Ward's *Big White Fog*, considered by Langston Hughes to be "the greatest, most encompassing play on Negro life that has ever been written," was an immediate box office hit when it opened in Chicago. But because of its depiction of black and white solidarity in the face of economic hard times, it was branded Communist propaganda and nervous FTP officials moved to shut it down.

While Jack Carter and Canada Lee went on to notable acting careers, it remains an unfortunate sign of the times that despite scores of energetic and critically lauded productions, the list of high-profile alumni to emerge from the FTP Negro units included few women or people of color.

Today, what remains of the African-American presence in FTP are production photographs, a few scripts, and words like these from the *Chicago Herald Examiner*'s review of *Big White Fog*: "It is a sheer joy to watch these Federal Theatre Negro players in action. Their voices are as sweet as honey. They are as much at ease on the stage as in their own homes."

The success of voodoo Macbeth encouraged Negro units across the country to adapt previously "white only" plays, such as Gilbert and Sullivan's The Mikado. *The all-black production, called* Swing Mikado, *was a hit in Chicago.*

RIVERA

Yes, Paris. Wild times. Come in.

ROCKEFELLER

I saw her today.

RIVERA

Yes.

RIVERA

So?

ROCKEFELLER

So. Oh, yes.

RIVERA

Some wine?

ROCKEFELLER

No. Anyway, I've chosen your sketch for mural composition for inclusion in the lobby of said Center de Rockefeller. The theme is "Man at the Crossroads Looking with Hope and High Vision to the Choosing of a New and Better Future." And we'd be thrilled to have you do it.

DIEGO

How much?

ROCKEFELLER

I'd like to propose a fee of $21,000 all inclusive, materials, assistants.

DIEGO

Would you like a drink?

INT. FED THEATRE OFFICES. DAY.

The beavers finish their play. The office applauds.

HALLIE

I think children are going to love this. When can you start rehearsal?

BEAVER MAN

Tomorrow.

HALLIE

Rose, will you put these two beavers in motion?

The beavers celebrate. Hallie exits.

DE ROHAN

Ask Harry for more money.

INT. WPA OFFICES. DAY.

Olive reaching the front of the line.

HAZEL HUFFMAN

Next.

OLIVE

That's me.

Blitzstein (Hank Azaria) is clubbed in the Union Square strike scene.

HUFFMAN
Name?

OLIVE
Olive Stanton.

HUFFMAN
Address.

OLIVE
I don't have one.

HUFFMAN
Are you currently employed?

OLIVE
No, ma'am.

HUFFMAN
You are applying for work in the Federal Theatre Project. What experience have you had in the theatre?

OLIVE
I sing on Broadway, I have sung on Broadway.

HUFFMAN
Last employer?

OLIVE
Huh?

HUFFMAN
Last employer, last producer of a show you were in so we can contact him.

OLIVE
He's dead.

Two Beavers put on a winning performance for the FTP staff.

HUFFMAN
His name?

OLIVE
Oh, Mr. Smith. Minsky Smith. You probably never heard of him; it was in Buffalo.

HUFFMAN
We can check.

OLIVE
Oh, never mind. There wasn't any Smith. I'm just a gal that needs a break is all. I've been walking the streets singing for nickels; I need a job. I can sing well; I'd work very hard.

HUFFMAN
Sister, this program is designed for theatre professionals who are out of work. We have limited resources; we can't possibly employ all the professionals; this isn't a Busby Berkeley fantasy, make you a star, kid, and all that.

OLIVE
Yes, I understand.

HUFFMAN
Are you strong?

OLIVE
Ma'am?

HUFFMAN
Are you strong? Can you lift things?

OLIVE

Yes, ma'am.

HUFFMAN

Project 891 needs a stagehand. You know what a stagehand does? Completely unglamorous push a broom, lift scenery, pull ropes kind of work. Are you interested?

OLIVE

Yes, ma'am. You bet.

HUFFMAN

You are not eligible for casting in any plays, understand?

OLIVE

Yes, ma'am.

HUFFMAN

Here's the address. Report tomorrow between 10 A.M. and 6 P.M.

OLIVE

Can I go today?

Olive Stanton finally reaches the FTP window. Emily Watson had a few things in common with the real-life Stanton, including time spent on welfare during her early years as an actor: "I had to go and sign on every week for my forty-five pounds [about seventy-five dollars]," says Watson. "It was pretty grim." She got off the dole only after her breakout role in Breaking the Waves *(1994).*

HUFFMAN

Go bananas.

INT. MAXINE ELLIOTT'S THEATRE (STAGE). DAY.

A meeting of cast and crew. The union representative, John Adair, is there.

WELLES

Sure if you're in a coal mine, a steel mill, a dangerous job, I can see the need for a break every hour or so. But this is theatre, this is not pouring slag; we are not risking our lives here.

ADAIR

The other side of that is working twenty hours a day for low wages, with no protections.

WELLES

These are actors we're talking about, not garment workers. This is not the Triangle Fire. No one is oppressing anyone here. We're just trying to get a show up. Once a show opens we work two hours a day. Easy street. Should management insist that you work an eight-hour day once the show is up? Ridiculous. Now if you don't mind, I'd like to get back to work.

HOUSEMAN

Bring in the puppets!

INT. JAIL. DAY.

Blitzstein sits behind bars in another world.

Above: The actor Jack Carter as Mephistopheles in the Welles-Houseman production of Faustus, *shown here with the Seven Deadly Sins puppets designed by Bil Baird. Below: In Robbins's re-creation of the 1937 play, Mephistopheles is played by the Broadway actor Chris McKinney. Matthew Owens created the puppets for the film.*

BLITZSTEIN
We're in a jail cell. Moll, our prostitute, sitting there, depressed, hungry. The door opens. And who walks in but the real whores. The crème de le crème of Steeltown. Doctor Specialist. The Editor of the Newspaper. The President of the University. Reverend Salvation.

BRECHT
And an artist or two. Don't forget they are the biggest whores.

BLITZSTEIN
Right. And they're in handcuffs. All been thrown in jail by some dolt cop. He made a mistake. Thought they were union organizers.

VOICE (LIBERTY #1)
Think of what my people would think if they could see me.

VOICE (LIBERTY #2)
Phone to Mr. Mister to come and bail us out.

BRECHT
Who is Mr. Mister?

BLITZSTEIN
He's the big cheese. He pulls the strings in
Steeltown.

Liberty Committee sings.

LIBERTY COMMITTEE
SO MR. MISTER, PLEASE TAKE PITY.
COME AND SAVE YOUR PET COMMITTEE
FROM DISASTER.

EXT. MAXINE ELLIOTT'S THEATRE. DUSK.
*Olive Stanton, address in hand, looks up at the marquee and
the address. She goes to the front, finds it open, and goes in.*

INT. HUFFMAN APARTMENT (HALLWAY). DAY.
Crickshaw knocks on the door. Hazel Huffman answers.

CRICKSHAW
I'm coming about the leaflet.

HUFFMAN
Yes.

CRICKSHAW
I'm here for the meeting.

HUFFMAN
Come in.

CRICKSHAW
I'm Tommy Crickshaw, ventriloquist.

HUFFMAN
OK. Did you bring your dummy?

CRICKSHAW
I prefer to think of him as a puppet. I never
leave him.

HUFFMAN
We're just getting started. Mr. Crickshaw, have
a seat.

*We move inside the apartment where five other disgruntled
workers wait. Huffman clears her throat, silences the throng.*

HUFFMAN
Good evening, ladies and gentlemen. My name is
Hazel Huffman. I thank you all for coming. I have
organized this meeting out of a deep concern for
what I see going on at my workplace and at other
sites where Federal Theatre exists. It is my hope
that tonight we can create a forum where people
can talk freely without fear of recrimination.
Don't worry. Powerful people are interested in
what we have to say. I know for a fact that there
are Congressmen who would like to know if
problems exist in the Federal Theatre. I for one
am ready to talk.

*Hazel Huffman (Joan Cusack), who was based on a real-life
WPA administrator, at her window.*

INT. MAXINE ELLIOTT'S THEATRE. DUSK.
*In the dim light of a lamp at the back of the house we see
Olive Stanton emerge. She walks to the back of the seats
and watches as the actors manipulate their puppets.*

CHANCE
They're scary.

SILVANO
They're sins.

CHANCE
Daddy, how come you're not doing a puppet?

SILVANO
Mr. Welles doesn't want me to.

JOEY
What part do you play?

SILVANO
The Fourth Scholar. It's a very important role.

INT. THEATRE (LIVING NEWSPAPER). DAY.
*An audience assembled. A buzz in the air, Harry Hopkins
sits beside Hallie.*

HARRY
Hello, my darling.

HALLIE
Hi, Harry.

HARRY
Hello. You know Paul Edwards?

HALLIE

Yes. Hello, Paul.

EDWARDS

Hallie.

HARRY

I'm sorry I'm late. Bridgeworker negotiations.

HALLIE

I trust Roosevelt is treating you well.

EDWARDS

Juggling three agencies, the bureaucratic wonder, "Harry Hopkins." Everything from cleaning children's teeth to controlling mosquitos.

HALLIE

Harry, what are these whispers I'm hearing about Congressman Dies?

HARRY

Whispers. It's a roar. He announces tomorrow a committee to investigate Communism in the WPA.

HALLIE

Oh, dear. Why didn't you tell me?

HARRY

I'm telling you. "Un-American Activities," he calls it. I wouldn't worry. Dies is a blowhard. This is just a bunch of politicians looking for headlines.

Flanagan, WPA director Harry Hopkins (Bob Balaban), and Paul Edwards (Ned Bellamy) take in an FTP production.

On Hallie, the lights dim; the show is beginning.

INT. HUFFMAN APARTMENT. DAY.

DISGRUNTLED WORKER #1

What about this mixed-race dating? Has anyone else noticed this happening in theatre groups?

SAUNDERS

I've noticed that the people at the Federal Theatre hobnob always with Negroes, throwing parties with them, left and right.

HUFFMAN

The problem I have personally with the WPA and with the arts projects in particular is that they seem to be run by people that are very elitist, very snobby-like.

CRICKSHAW

I've noticed this too. Personally I don't think there's any room to advance, if you don't agree with them, if you're not the same as them, in politics, if you don't have politic-wise the same mind, and besides, Reds aren't funny. I just don't think that they're funny.

HUFFMAN

Exactly my point, Mr. Crickshaw. For example, I am aware of a very talented playwright who has had his production canceled in favor of a much more political work. It is outrageous. The main criteria in this project is not art but who you

know. I am an outspoken person. I have been denied promotions because of my beliefs.

Crickshaw nods. He's hooked.

INT. RIVERA APARTMENT. DUSK.
Diego dances with Frida Kahlo. Rockefeller dances with the models. They are obviously drunk.

INT. HUFFMAN APARTMENT. DUSK.
The meeting continues. Huffman and Crickshaw exchange glances. Could this be love?

> HUFFMAN
Punch, Mr. Crickshaw?

> CRICKSHAW
Yes. Thank you very much, Miss Huffman.

INT. JAIL. DAY.
Blitzstein acts out his play in his head as he sits in a lotus position on the floor of the jail cell.

> BLITZSTEIN
Oh boy, I've just been grilled.

> EVA
Who's that?

> BLITZSTEIN
Larry Foreman, the union leader.

> EVA
I like this, Marc.

Coworkers gather at Huffman's apartment to discuss their dissatisfaction with the Federal Theatre. In the center is Mary Robbins, the director's mother.

> BLITZSTEIN
He comes into the jail cell and sees all these rich people sitting there.

> BLITZSTEIN
What's the whole Liberty Committee doing here in the pokey and on the wrong side of the bars?

> VOICE (LIBERTY #1)
That's the man you want.

> VOICE (LIBERTY #2)
He's a Red, an agitator.

> BLITZSTEIN
Mr. Mister tries to bribe him, but he tells him to get lost. He won't sell out his union. His people are marching on the jail.

> BLITZSTEIN (AND LARRY FOREMAN) (V.O.)
THAT'S THUNDER, THAT'S LIGHTNING,
AND IT'S GOING TO SURROUND YOU!
NO WONDER THOSE STORMBIRDS
SEEM TO CIRCLE AROUND YOU. . . .
WELL, YOU CAN'T CLIMB DOWN,
AND YOU CAN'T SIT STILL;
THAT'S A STORM THAT'S GOING TO
        LAST UNTIL . . .

INT. MAXINE ELLIOTT'S THEATRE. DAY.

Title: FOUR MONTHS LATER, WINTER 1937

We start on Olive Stanton in the audience watching. Blitzstein is singing "Cradle Will Rock" to Hallie, De Rohan, Welles, Houseman, and the entire company of Project 891.

BLITZSTEIN
THE FINAL WIND BLOWS . . .
AND WHEN THE WIND BLOWS,
THE CRADLE WILL ROCK!

Applause from the company.

HALLIE
Well I think it's terrific, Jack. Marc, you've written something groundbreaking here. Never before, to my knowledge, has an American musical dealt with content, social issues, dramatic themes. You're reinventing musical theatre. Orson, don't overdesign this. Keep it pure. Keep it simple.

WELLES
You've got my word, Madam Flanagan.

HALLIE
I'll be checking in.

WELLES
Congratulations, Marc. Auditions are tonight at six. The score will be left with a pianist today if anyone wants to learn the songs.

Welles walks briskly towards the exit.

HOUSEMAN
Thank you, boys and girls.

WELLES
Augusta, did you make the reservation at "21"?

AUGUSTA
Yes, Orson.

WELLES
Jack, Marc, come with me. Mrs. Flanagan, will you join us?

HALLIE
"21"? Too rich for my blood. I can see the headlines, "Civil Servant Dining at '21' on Your Tax Dollars."

WELLES
The perils of officialdom.

CANADA LEE
So what does a Negro actor play in this all-white play?

WELLES
All-white? Ridiculous. You'll play the Reverend Salvation.

CANADA LEE
A white Protestant Minister?

WELLES
In makeup. In a world of Amos and Andy, you can play a white Protestant. Makeup, my friend. Subversion.

Olive Stanton approaches John Houseman as he walks towards the exit.

OLIVE
Mr. Houseman, I'm Olive Stanton.

HOUSEMAN
I know you.

OLIVE
I'm a stagehand.

HOUSEMAN
You're a stagehand.

OLIVE
I would like to, with your permission, sir, if it would be possible to audition?

HOUSEMAN
For *Cradle Will Rock*? I don't know.

EXT. MAXINE ELLIOTT'S THEATRE. DAY.
De Rohan walks with Hallie. It is snowing.

DE ROHAN
Are you crazy? We're being investigated by Congress. We can't do this play, Hallie.

HALLIE
Why not?

DE ROHAN
Greedy industrialist brought down by the working man?

HALLIE
It's pro-union, yes, but so is our audience.

DE ROHAN
A stage full of marching workers trample the capitalist.

HALLIE
They don't trample him.

DE ROHAN
It's an attack on capitalism.

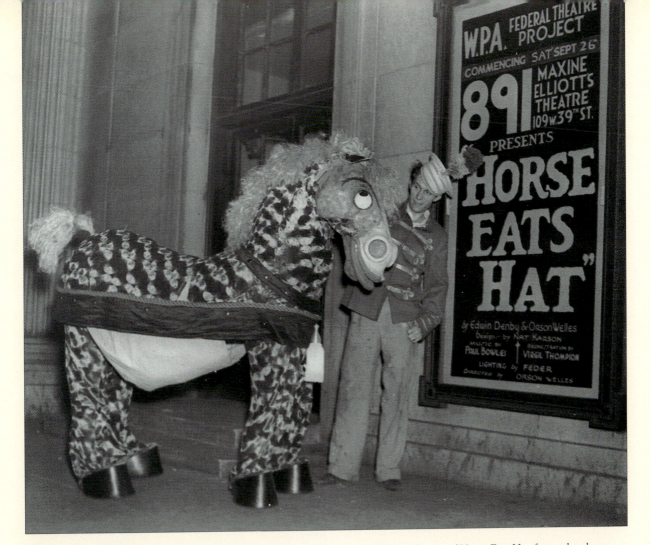

Riding high on the success of the voodoo *Macbeth* production, Houseman won Hallie Flanagan's approval to set up a "classical theatre unit" with his enfant terrible partner, Welles. Wanting to avoid titles with stuffy words like repertory, Houseman named the new unit Project 891, after the last three digits of the string of numbers on the WPA contract that named him its managing producer. In mid-1936, he moved the company into Maxine Elliott's Theatre on West 39th Street.

For Project 891's first production, Welles and Edwin Denby jazzed up a nineteenth-century French farce to give it maximum Depression-era audience appeal. The result was *Horse Eats Hat*, a fast-paced extravaganza that, according to the *New York Times*, lacked "a beginning and an end [or] rhyme and reason." But the show delivered exuberant, slapstick humor based on a sequence of snowballing absurdities that began with a devoured chapeau and culminated with the hero—and the owner of the offending horse—being chased through the streets and boudoirs of Paris by a pistol-firing mob of citizenry and gendarmes.

The lead role of Freddie was a first Broadway success for Joseph Cotten, who went on to act in *Citizen Kane*—a thinly veiled and trenchant portrait of William Randolph Hearst—considered by many to be Welles's cinematic masterpiece. The production also drew on the talents of Bil Baird who created the two-person "horse," the rear half of which was

Project 891's production of Horse Eats Hat *featured orchestration by Virgil Thomson, lighting by Abe Feder, a lead performance by Joseph Cotten, and the hat-eating star, the rear end of which Welles ordered to fall into the orchestra pit each night.*

designed to pratfall nightly into the orchestra pit. Baird also built the extraordinary puppets for Project 891's next experiment, *Dr. Faustus,* and later achieved considerable success with his own marionette theatre.

While writers like Marc Connelly and John Dos Passos wept with laughter at the horse's antics, not every audience member was amused. What one reviewer saw as "a work of genuine theatre art played in a cloud of dust [at] a tempo that leaves art, life, audience, and sometimes the actors behind it," the young conservative congressman Everett Dirksen viewed as "salacious tripe." Records show that less than three years later, it was Dirksen who led the call from the house floor to defund the FTP.

A Departure from "Classical" Theatre

HALLIE

Not at all. It's an attack on greed. It's a good play—it's funny, it's moving, the music is great. Stop fretting, Pierre.

Welles exits the theatre with Blitzstein & Housman.

WELLES

I see glass.

BLITZSTEIN

Glass?

WELLES

Don't ask me why, but there is something about standing on a surface of glass, the risk of it, the potential for injury. It would be completely safe of course, thick glass, safe, thick glass. *The Cradle Will Rock* is spectacular.

INT. TAXI. DAY.

BLITZSTEIN

Glass?

WELLES

A stage of glass, yes. Tell me, are you a Communist?

HOUSEMAN

Perhaps we should talk about the auditions, what we are looking for in each of the roles.

WELLES

Marc, are you a Red?

BLITZSTEIN

Officially, no. I am a homosexual and that excludes me from membership in the party. I am faithful to the ideals of the party.

WELLES

I am faithful to the party of ideas.

HOUSEMAN

You are faithful to the idea of a party. Any party.

WELLES

Sparkling wit, Jack. I thought you were married, Marc.

BLITZSTEIN

My wife passed away last year.

INT. ROCKEFELLER CENTER LOBBY. DAY.

Diego Rivera paints. The mural has progressed considerably. Rockefeller enters.

Houseman, Augusta, Welles, and Flanagan respond to an early run-through of Marc Blitzstein's The Cradle Will Rock.

Project 891's dynamic duo could not have sprung from more disparate roots. Born in Bucharest in 1902, "Jack" Houseman (né Jacques Haussmann) grew up speaking several languages, and early on manifested an attraction to theatre and a talent for business.

Heavily invested in the international grain trade, Houseman was wiped out in the crash of '29, which he took as an opportunity to commit himself to theatre. Captivated by Welles's presence as Tybalt in Katharine Cornell's production of *Romeo and Juliet*, Houseman cast the barely-twenty-year-old actor as a J. P. Morgan–type robber baron in Archibald MacLeish's verse play *Panic* in 1935. What Houseman referred to as their "marriage" had begun.

Born in Wisconsin in 1915 to a musically talented mother and an alcoholic father, Orson Welles was encouraged to develop his precocious talents. In Barbara Leaming's biography, Welles describes how "the word *genius* was whispered into my ear, the first thing I ever heard while I was still mewling in the crib, so it never occurred to me that I wasn't until middle age."

At sixteen Welles traveled to Ireland, where, underage by two years, he lied his way into Dublin's Gate Theatre Company. Returning to the United States from his apprenticeship, he met Thornton Wilder in Chicago and was in turn introduced to Katharine Cornell, who cast him in *Romeo and Juliet*. Welles's actress wife Virginia also served as his not-so-silent creative partner and is credited with suggesting *Macbeth*'s relocation to Haiti. She also

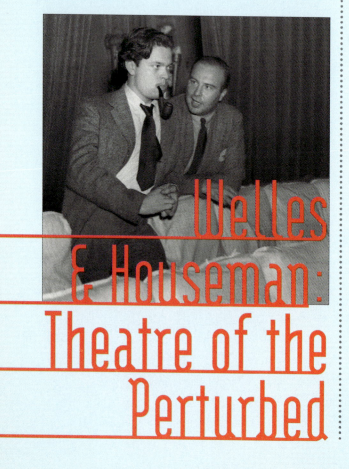

Welles & Houseman: Theatre of the Perturbed

maintained an abiding suspicion that Houseman would betray her husband in the manner of *Othello*'s Iago.

But the volatile relationship between producer and director worked, fueled simultaneously by Welles's need for an older facilitator and Houseman's awe of "this astonishing boy whose theatre experience was so much greater and richer than mine—it was I who was the pupil and he the teacher."

In the aftermath of *The Cradle Will Rock*, Welles resigned from Project 891, and Flanagan, to her regret, was forced to fire Houseman. But Welles was hardly one to passively accept the status quo. Frustrated by bureaucratic delays in funding, he had subsidized Project 891 out of his own radio work as the voice of the "Shadow" and other commercial ventures. So it wasn't long before he proposed to Houseman, "Why the hell don't we start a theatre of our own?"

The resulting Mercury Theatre presented Shakespeare's *Julius Caesar* and restaged *Cradle* and *War of the Worlds*, a radio broadcast that caused a national panic when listeners mistook H. G. Wells's fantasy for an actual news report of an invasion by Martians.

But the emotional costs of this brilliant collaboration increasingly took their toll. Houseman began to feel that his "two main functions were, first, to supply Orson, beyond the limits of prudence and reason, with the human and material elements he required for his creative work, and second, to shield him not only from outside interference, but even more, from the intense pressures of his own destructive nature."

For Welles, resentment for his controlling partner was also coming to a boil. In his memoir *This Is Orson Welles* (cowritten with Peter Bogdanovich), he confessed that Houseman was "one of the few subjects that depresses me so deeply that it really spoils my day to think of him." Their set-to's grew so violent that at one point Welles reportedly heaved cans of flaming sterno at Houseman's retreating back.

In 1939, RKO Pictures made Welles a dream offer: come to Hollywood and write, direct, and star in any movie you want to make. Houseman, now on his own, directed Broadway productions of Stephen Vincent Benét's *Devil and Daniel Webster* and worked with Cornell on a stage adaptation of Richard Wright's novel *Native Son*. He achieved on-screen stardom late in life in the role of a tyrannical professor in the 1973 film *The Paper Chase*, for which he won the Oscar for Best Supporting Actor.

Though he briefly collaborated with Welles on what would become the script for the universally lauded *Citizen Kane*, it is an indication of how deeply alienated these once-inseparable partners had become that Houseman never received credit for his contribution from the man he once considered "the rightful and undisputed master" of the American stage.

Orson Welles and John Houseman swap ideas during a break in Horse Eats Hat. *Despite their complex and often tumultuous relationship, the two formed the most innovative and successful team in the Federal Theatre.*

ROCKEFELLER
Are you getting everything you need, Diego?

RIVERA
I need burnt cyprus embers.

ROCKEFELLER
I'll send someone.

A pause.

ROCKEFELLER
You know, at first I had unrealistic expectations,
Diego. I'm glad you are taking your time now.
Certainly Michelangelo took his time on the
Sistine Chapel.

DIEGO
I work three months now. Not much.

ROCKEFELLER
I've come to understand art more with this
experience.

A pause.

ROCKEFELLER
What is that emanating from the man in the
center?

DIEGO
This is the recombination of atoms and the
division of a cell. Those are cells, germs,
bacteria; the wonders of the microscope.

ROCKEFELLER
I see. It's fascinating and so modern.

A pause.

*Angus Macfadyen and Cary Elwes as Orson Welles and John
Houseman. "During the shoot, we went to a few very expensive
restaurants together as Orson and Jack," Macfadyen explained.
"Cary had to suffer the brunt of this joyously anarchic character"
that Macfadyen became. "It caused some friction between us as
actors, but we used it to feed the love-hate relationship we were
trying to capture. It also culminated in our not talking to one
another for an entire week at the end of the shoot."*

ROCKEFELLER
These well-dressed people over here, what is that?

RIVERA
What do you see?

ROCKEFELLER
Oh, I get it. Picasso played this game with me. I
see society at a party of some kind.

RIVERA
That's it. The debauched rich. Above their heads
is a syphilis cell.

ROCKEFELLER
The rich in general?

RIVERA
No, in specific.

ROCKEFELLER
You don't mean me?

RIVERA
You don't have syphilis, do you?

ROCKEFELLER
No, of course not.

A pause.

51

ROCKEFELLER
And this is a war of some kind?

RIVERA
A battlefield with men in the holocaust of war and next to it unemployed workers being clubbed by police. You like it?

INT. MAXINE ELLIOTT'S THEATRE STAGE. DAY.
Silvano works with the pianist on a song. As he finishes and exits we find John Adair and Olive Stanton.

ADAIR
Olive, isn't it?

OLIVE
Yes.

ADAIR
I'm John Adair.

OLIVE
I know. You're a great actor. I've been watching you.

ADAIR
Thanks.

OLIVE
Did you like the play?

ADAIR
I thought it was interesting. I like it. I felt it could have gone farther. How do you stand on Spain?

OLIVE
I . . . I'm not sure.

ADAIR
Did you just crawl out from a rock? I'm just kidding. A lot of people don't know. Spain is being attacked by Fascists from Italy and Nazis from Germany.

Marvel looks above him in the rafters of the theatre where Geer and Sandra are making love.

MARVEL
Oh to be young.

BERT
Is that what I think?

DULCE
Yes.

BERT
They're at it again.

DULCE
Like bunnies. God bless them.

MARVEL
O what a bursting out there was
And what a blossoming
When we had all the summertime
And she had all the spring.

Back to John Adair and Olive Stanton.

ADAIR
Roosevelt isn't doing anything 'cause he thinks the Spanish are with Russia.

OLIVE
Oh, okay. That's terrible. I don't know so much. I had no idea. I thought that we were talking about the play.

ADAIR
We were.

OLIVE
I liked it. Made me think.

ADAIR
Uh oh.

OLIVE
About unions, and how important they are. I guess I don't know too much about Spain, though.

ADAIR
So I gather.

OLIVE
Or politics.

ADAIR
What about dancing? Do you know the wonderful world of dancing?

OLIVE
Here? In front of everyone?

ADAIR
Why not? You want to audition, don't you? You can't be shy.

OLIVE
I'm working.

ADAIR
Union break. Fifteen minutes.

OLIVE
Are you asking me to dance?

ADAIR
Yes, ma'am.

Extras take a break between scenes in Madison Square.

Faustian Proportions

With its next production, Project 891 went back to the classics, sort of. With their restaging of Christopher Marlowe's *Tragicall History of Doctor Faustus*, Welles and Houseman again brought theatergoers into the dark, magical heart of Elizabethan drama. Originally intended as a two-week filler, *Dr. Faustus* ended up playing to full houses for five months. In addition to directing, Welles cast himself in the title role as the doomed metaphysician who pays for short-lived earthly power with the coin of his soul.

Much of the production's extraordinary theatrical energy may be laid to parallels, both real and imagined, between the mythical doctor and the play's brilliant young director. In his memoir, Houseman—an admittedly biased observer—recalled that "there were moments when Faustus seemed to be expressing, through Marlowe's words, some of Orson's personal agony and private terror. Orson was sure he was doomed, rarely free of a sense of sin and a fear of retribution so intense and immediate that it drove him to seek refuge in debauchery or work."

And it is certainly true that aspects of the Project 891 production reflected Welles's sensibility at its "Faustian" extreme. His treatment of the play called for hundreds of cues, many of them split second. Ferocious pyrotechnics nearly prompted the fire department to shut down the theatre. And Actors' Equity representatives locked horns with Welles over rehearsals that routinely dragged into the wee hours. But despite what Houseman called "satanic complications," *Dr. Faustus* proved one of the most iconoclastic, and successful, productions the FTP ever mounted.

In *Arena*, Flanagan offered this eloquent insider's view:

> Going into the Maxine Elliott during rehearsals was like going into the pit of hell: total darkness punctuated by stabs of light, trapdoors opening and closing to reveal bewildered stagehands or actors going up and down, and around in circles; explosions; properties disappearing in a clap of thunder; and onstage Orson, muttering the mighty lines and interspersing them with fierce adjurations to the invisible but omnipresent Feder. The only point of equilibrium in these midnight séances was Jack Carter, quiet, slightly amused, probably the only actor who ever played Mephistopheles without raising his voice.

Above: Orson Welles as Doctor Faustus in the 1937 Welles-Houseman production of Marlowe's play. It was the young producer's first leading role on the stage. Left: Angus Macfadyen as Orson Welles playing Doctor Faustus in Robbins's film.

❝The legend of the man who sells his soul to the devil in exchange for knowledge and power and who must finally pay for his brief triumph with the agonies of personal damnation was uncomfortably close to the shape of Welles's own personal myth.❞

—John Houseman

Indeed, Carter's dignified, self-contained portrayal of the devil's emissary made a brilliant counterpoint to Welles's volatile Faustus, and was noted by the *New York Times* as a "successful example of integrated casting." The play also cemented Abe Feder's growing reputation as pioneer in lighting design and brought acclaim for Bil Baird's powerful stage puppetry.

The play opened to rave reviews in January 1937. According to Houseman, when Harry Hopkins came backstage to greet the exhausted, yet triumphant, company, he innocently asked the director and producer if they were having a good time in the Federal Theatre. They were too dumbfounded to answer anything but yes.

CORNELIUS

Welles's utter absorption in the production of Faustus extended to designing all of the actors' costumes himself.

OLIVE
Then ask.

ADAIR
Miss Stanton, will you do me the honor?

They begin to dance. Slow, romantic.

INT. "21" RESTAURANT. DAY.
A very fancy, upscale restaurant. Welles, Blitzstein, and Houseman enter.

BLITZSTEIN
Am I supposed to be impressed?

WELLES
No.

HOUSEMAN
The temptations of Satan, Marc.

WELLES
Are you calling me Satan, Jack?

BLITZSTEIN
So you'll fill my belly with rich foods, fine wine, and I will understand better the sacred aims of Orson Welles. In my sated state I will give myself over to you.

WELLES
I'm not talking about me. I'm talking about the follies of politics. We can talk about it over a frankfurter if you like.

HOUSEMAN
We can also talk about the play.

We find Sarfatti sitting at a table with Mathers, Hearst, and the Countess.

SARFATTI
What is the prevailing wisdom here?

MATHERS
Sometime next month.

HEARST
The League of Nations are applying pressure.

MATHERS
All of a sudden everyone cares about Ethiopia. All of a sudden Haile Selassie is an intelligent rational leader.

SARFATTI
Doing business with you has been important to us. An embargo will be so harmful.

HEARST
Another example of rampant socialism run amok in this administration.

MATHERS
Perhaps the best thing to do is to stockpile in anticipation of the worst.

The camera moves to find Blitzstein, Welles, and Houseman sitting at a table.

BLITZSTEIN
Let's talk about prostitution and your connection with it.

WELLES
Do you have evidence?

BLITZSTEIN
Not of the loins, of the soul.

WELLES
Oh, boy.

INT. FEDERAL THEATRE OFFICES. DAY.
Hallie bounds in, full of energy. The radio plays. O'Hara listens with De Rohan.

The poster for the Welles-Houseman production of Faustus stands out for its graphic impact. Its central image is a virulent green skeleton taken from Albrecht Dürer's Dance of Death.

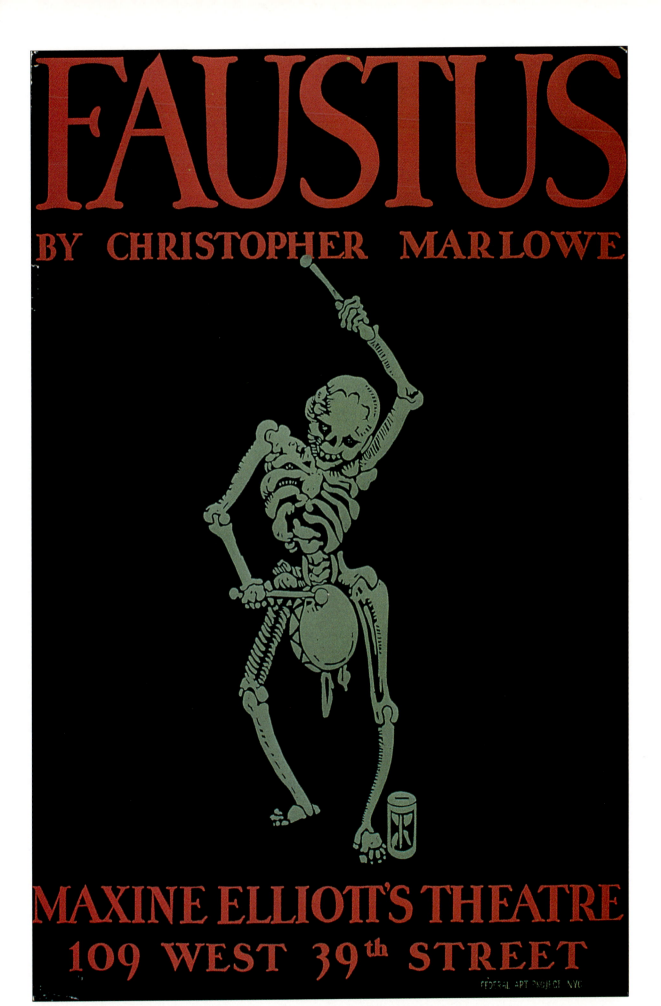

In *Mark the Music: The Life and Work of Marc Blitzstein*, biographer Eric Gordon called *Cradle* a "thoroughly American work, not just in theme and in its tunes, but in the way Blitzstein wrote and set to music the speech patterns of a wide gamut of social classes." But the class Blitzstein most wanted to inspire was the working class—by creating "art that will bring it to a deeper knowledge of itself, and reality that will show a possible new reality."

In *Cradle*, rendered in a larger-than-life cartoon style, this new reality was forged through the victory of incorruptible industrial workers and their even more downtrodden allies, represented by Moll, a distinctly unwilling hooker who laments:

> I ain't in Steeltown long,
> I work two days a week;
> The other five my efforts ain't required.
> For two days out of seven,
> Two dollar bills I'm given.
> So I'm just searchin' along the street,
> For on those five days it's nice to eat.

Blitzstein also drew on the epic theatre techniques of his German mentor Bertolt Brecht, who exaggerated characters into purposeful distortions for dramatic effect. In his first draft of *Cradle*, Blitzstein named his bitter adversaries John L. Lewis and Mr. Morgan (after the legendary banker and industrialist). In the final version, they emerged as the archetypal Larry Foreman, pitted against the faceless Mr. Mister. Like Flanagan, John Houseman saw *The Cradle Will Rock*'s totality as exceeding the sum of its parts—its style falling "somewhere between realism, vaudeville, and oratory."

Even the mainstream press accorded *Cradle* largely favorable notices. The *Herald Tribune* called it a "savagely humorous social cartoon with music that hits hard and sardonically," while the *New York Times* saw a play "written with extraordinary versatility and played with enormous gusto, the best thing militant labor has put into the theatre yet." The then-liberal *Post* pronounced *Cradle* a "propagandistic tour de force," comparable to Clifford Odets's classic 1935 *Waiting for Lefty*.

Under fire for promoting revolution in the guise of "relief," Hallie Flanagan stuck to her guns, affirming that "the theatre, when it's good, is always dangerous."

The Cradle Rocks!

For their next act, the Welles-Houseman team served audiences a bubbling social cauldron of contemporary American class struggle. In producing Marc Blitzstein's *Cradle Will Rock*, they raised the dramatic stakes, and upped the political ante as well.

Hallie Flanagan, for her part, knew and acknowledged the risks that came with giving the government's de facto seal of approval to the militantly pro-union play. But as she recalled in *Arena*, "It took no wizardry to see that this was not a play set to music, but a music-plus-play equaling something new and better than either."

But no one, including Flanagan, could have anticipated the coincidence of *Cradle*'s premiere with a real-life "Steeltown" bloodbath, recounted by Houseman as "a double accident of timing that would project us all onto the front pages of the nation's press. What Hallie had taken for a dynamic piece of Americana had turned into a time bomb that threatened to bring the entire project tumbling about her head."

Above left: Marc Blitzstein (Hank Azaria) composes The Cradle Will Rock *at the piano.*
Above: The original program for Cradle.

O'HARA

How was *Cradle?*

HALLIE

Very good. Funny.

DE ROHAN

It's a nightmare.

O'HARA

Why?

HALLIE

It's pro-union. How's the inquisition going?

O'HARA

I just don't understand. All of the people that are testifying sound nuts. Loony.

HALLIE

Take notes. Are the reviews of the *Revolt of the Beavers* in?

O'HARA

No.

HALLIE

Let me know when they come.

Off the radio we hear:

SALLY SAUNDERS (V.O.)

The day before I had noticed a Negro making a sketch of me as I was dancing. He shoved the sketch in my face. I did not know anything about him. All I knew was that a Negro had sketched me.

CHAIRMAN DIES (V.O.)

After that time when he asked permission to make . . .

INT. VAUDEVILLE DRESSING ROOM. DAY.

Off the radio we hear:

CHAIRMAN DIES (V.O.)

(continued) . . . a date with you, did you report it to the supervisor?

SAUNDERS (V.O.)

She said she felt very sorry that I felt that way about it because she personally encouraged Negro attention on all occasions and went out with them or with any Negro who asked her to.

We move off of the radio to see Huffman listening with Crickshaw to the testimony.

HUFFMAN

They're getting it all wrong. Their emphasis is on morals not politics. Don't they understand that everybody lusts? They are not going to stop the corruption in the program because people are fornicating in it. This is about Communism, not immoral procreation.

CRICKSHAW

I agree, Hazel.

Kindred souls Hazel Huffman (Joan Cusack) and Tommy Crickshaw (Bill Murray) listen to radio testimony given before the Dies Committee.

HUFFMAN

I must get called for this committee.

CRICKSHAW

You would be fantastic.

A knock on the door. It opens to reveal Sid and Larry, the apprentices.

SID

Mr. Crickshaw?

CRICKSHAW

Yes.

LARRY

Is it time for our tutorial?

CRICKSHAW

I can't come right now. Tutorial is canceled today. Work on your own and I'll review.

LARRY

Can we use the stage?

CRICKSHAW

Sure, sure, go ahead.

INT. "21" RESTAURANT. DAY.

BLITZSTEIN

How long can you whore your talents before you're used up, unwanted?

WELLES

Whore my talents?

BLITZSTEIN

Who is the sponsor of *The Shadow*?

WELLES

Think of them as my patrons.

HOUSEMAN

Your corporate Medicis.

WELLES

They pay well, Marc. And with that money I pay for theatre. I buy props that the Federal Government won't approve, costumes, makeup, set pieces, puppets. I feed my friends and get my actors drunk.

HOUSEMAN

You are such a god, Orson.

The composer Blitzstein (Hank Azaria), haunted throughout the film by the ghosts of his late wife Eva Goldbeck (Susan Heimbinder) and his mentor Bertolt Brecht (Stephen Skybell). "Tim and I worked out a very specific way of dealing with the ghosts," says Azaria.

More than thirty-five years after his death, Marcus Samuel Blitzstein remains as compelling and enigmatic a figure as any on America's stage. Born March 2, 1905, to a Philadelphia banking family, Blitzstein revealed his musical talents early. By the age of seven he was playing Mozart piano concerti and studying under teachers trained by Liszt and Tchaikovsky.

In his early twenties, Blitzstein traveled to Europe to study with the renowned composers Nadia Boulanger and Arnold Schoenberg. While there, however, he became more drawn toward the expressionist, discordantly jazzy works of Kurt Weill and other composers in the Songspeil style, although initially he had dismissed them as "crude."

Back in New York in 1935 and increasingly convinced that "music must have a social base," Blitzstein met Weill's longtime collaborator, German dramatist Bertolt Brecht. Brecht heard an early version of "Nickel under the Foot"—later to become *Cradle*'s showstopper—and liked it. And yet, "he said if I was serious I must make prostitution a dramatic symbol for overall prostitution—the press, the church, the courts, the arts—contemporary man's sellout of his talent, his soul, and dignity." Rising to Brecht's challenge, Blitzstein wrote the rest of *Cradle* in a frenzied two months and dedicated it to his mentor.

In the film *Cradle Will Rock*, Brecht is depicted as recurrent hallucination, provoking and ultimately affirming Blitzstein's achievement. Also offering encouragement is the ghost of Blitzstein's wife, Eva Goldbeck, a novelist and Brecht translator whom, despite his homosexuality, Blitzstein had fallen in love with and married in 1933. His grief over her death just three years later helped propel the frenetic pace with which he completed his masterpiece, which fellow FTP composer Virgil Thomson called "prophetic and confident," full of "sweetness, a cutting wit, inexhaustible fancy, and faith."

Post-*Cradle*, Blitzstein continued to bring his talents to the labor stage. But with the outbreak of World War II, he joined the army. He returned to Broadway in 1949 with a

Blitzstein: Composer & Enigma

How many fakers,

Peace undertakers,

Paid strike breakers,

How many toiling, ailing,

Dying, piled-up bodies, Brother,

Does it take to make you wise?

----from *The Cradle Will Rock*

musical version of Lillian Hellman's *The Little Foxes*. In 1952, in the teeth of the postwar Red scare, Blitzstein wrote an English adaptation of *Threepenny Opera*, presenting the legendary Brecht-Weill collaboration to American audiences for the first time. Opening in New York in 1954 with Weill's widow, Lotte Lenya, leading a brilliant cast, the show immediately proved a critical and box office success.

Brecht's *Threepenny Opera* was a modern-day fable peopled by prostitutes, swindlers, and a corrupt police chief whose old army buddy is the criminal Macheath. Popularly known as "Mack the Knife," Brecht's gangster-hero wore "fancy gloves" to do his dirty work, "so there's never a trace of red." The ballad Weill wrote for Mack turned surprisingly into a hit song—to be performed by scores of musical artists, including Ella Fitzgerald, Louis Armstrong, Eartha Kitt, and Bobby Darin.

In 1958, four years after his triumph with *Threepenny Opera*, Blitzstein was called to testify before Senator Joseph McCarthy's House Un-American Activities Committee. He admitted his former membership in the Communist Party, but unlike several notable entertainment figures, he refused to name names. Although famous and well-heeled thanks to *Threepenny* royalties, Blitzstein remained semi-reclusive in his later years. He never moved out of the tiny studio apartment on East 12th Street where he had first sketched out the chords to *Cradle* on a well-worn upright piano.

In 1964, after a bout of heavy drinking on holiday in Martinique, Blitzstein was severely beaten in a back alley by three sailors and died soon afterward. Whether his murder was a result of gay bashing, a robbery gone awry, or a combination of both is impossible to know for sure. What is certain, though, is how deeply Blitzstein's influence pervades American musical theatre to this day. He is, as Leonard Bernstein once called him, "irreplaceable." Today, shades of *Cradle* may be glimpsed in socially oriented musicals from *Les Misérables* to *Kiss of the Spider Woman*.

Marc Blitzstein, around the time he wrote The Cradle Will Rock.

WELLES

There's nothing wrong with money, Marc. Everyone digs that beat, wants in. It's all the rage. Even the boys in the Kremlin are starting to roll around in it. You think that Mr. Stalin is eating the same meal as the factory worker? We call it the Ritz, you call it the Comintern Club.

BLITZSTEIN

I have no problem with money. I need it just like everyone else does. The question is what will you do for money? Where do you draw the line? *Cradle Will Rock* is about prostitution. Prostitution of education, prostitution of the press, the courts, and most important for you and me, prostitution of the artist. Where do you draw the line, Orson? Or do you draw the line?

HOUSEMAN

Well, this is going extremely well.

The Countess approaches Houseman, Welles, and Blitzstein.

COUNTESS

Jack.

HOUSEMAN

Hello, darling.

COUNTESS

I hope you don't mind me interrupting. I was frightfully bored at my table and thoroughly excluded.

HOUSEMAN

Sit down, sit down. We were just creating an insurmountable tension for our working relationship.

INT. SILVANO APARTMENT. DAY.
Silvano hears children's voices as he turns a corner.

SILVANO

Birthday Boy.

His son Joey runs to him.

JOEY

Papa. I'm so happy you're here.

And he runs off to rejoin his game. Silvano's mother approaches.

MAMA

You're late for your own child's birthday.

SILVANO

I had to learn a song. I have an audition tonight.

A besotted Crickshaw helps Huffman rehearse her testimony.

UNCLE

With Welles. How's Orson Welles doing?

MARTA

"The Shadow" knows.

She giggles.

INT. VAUDEVILLE THEATRE DRESSING ROOM. DAY.
Hazel is rehearsing her testimony with Crickshaw and dummy.

HUFFMAN (V.O.)

Yes, Congressman Dies, The Living Newspaper is the name of the project. They write nothing else but propaganda plays.

CRICKSHAW

They write the plays that are produced by the theatre project?

62

HUFFMAN
Yes, sir.

DUMMY
And they produce them too?

HUFFMAN
They write them and they produce them.

DUMMY
They are on the Federal payroll?

HUFFMAN
They are on the Federal payroll, each one. I don't know about this.

DUMMY
You don't know about this.

HUFFMAN
I don't mean to be rude but this is distracting.

DUMMY
Distracting?

HUFFMAN
Can you stop him?

DUMMY
Stop me?

HUFFMAN
Yes, you.

DUMMY
What gives?

HUFFMAN
Please, Mr. Crickshaw.

DUMMY
No, Tommy.

HUFFMAN
I would rather just do it with you. Can we be alone?

CRICKSHAW
Me.

HUFFMAN
Yes.

CRICKSHAW
Just me?

HUFFMAN
Yes.

CRICKSHAW
I can do the Congressman. *(he puts dummy down)* I beg your pardon, Miss Huffman. Please continue.

INT. MAXINE ELLIOTT'S THEATRE. DAY.
Cast members learn a song. Olive and John Adair.

OLIVE
The truth is I don't think of anything when I'm singing. I'm in a happy place. I don't think of how hungry I am, or cold. I can even be singing about sad things and I feel all lifted up.

ADAIR
You love to sing.

OLIVE
Yes, that's it.

ADAIR
It makes you warm. It makes you forget.

Pause.

ADAIR *(cont'd)*
You have beautiful eyes.

OLIVE

Oh.

ADAIR

Why were you crying before?

OLIVE

When?

ADAIR

When we danced. Was I that bad a dancer?

OLIVE

No. It was nothing.

ADAIR

You're holding onto secrets, Olive Stanton.

OLIVE

What?

ADAIR

There's things that have happened to you. Bad things.

OLIVE

I guess I'm just not used to kindness lately. You took me by surprise.

ADAIR

We've all been hit by it, Olive. We've all been hungry. No one here is going to judge you. This is your family now.

Rockefeller enlists Margherita Sarfatti's support in "cheering up" Diego Rivera's mural.

INT. "21" RESTAURANT. DAY.
Rockefeller sits with Sarfatti.

ROCKEFELLER

Well, my official position is that I love it. I am thrilled. I think it is in my best interest to publicly be excited, but like I said, I have trepidation about this mural. First of all, it's not great art.

SARFATTI

It will be great. It is not finished yet.

ROCKEFELLER

It's not Picasso. It's not Matisse.

SARFATTI

They said no to you. They didn't want to paint your lobby. Diego did. You are not going to get anywhere attacking the quality of the art. First of all, you're wrong. Second of all, you can't win. There will always be a prominent art critic to call you a boor, an unfeeling, unsympathetic capitalist blockhead incapable of seeing true art. I know that is not you, Nelson.

ROCKEFELLER

Will you talk to him? See if you can cheer it up just a little.

SARFATTI

Cheer it up?

ROCKEFELLER

Margherita, there are microscopic cells of bubonic plague on the walls of my lobby.

The camera moves to find Welles's table.

BLITZSTEIN

If that's the way you feel, why do *Cradle Will Rock*?

WELLES

Because it will piss off all the right people. And when you piss people off in the theatre, you're doing something right. Theatre should provoke, not pander. People should leave the theatre wanting to fight, to jump, to argue, to fuck. Damn it, Marc, if people leave *Cradle* and head for a bistro for Spanish coffee and a cigarette to discuss the intellectual underpinnings of our story, then we are dead men. I want angry, lust-filled theatregoers.

COUNTESS

Here, here.

They laugh and toast. Blitzstein less amused than others. Mathers and Hearst hover.

INT. VAUDEVILLE THEATRE DRESSING ROOM. DAY.

HUFFMAN

They had another play called *Processional*. It dealt with a miner who had torn up the American flag and was put into jail. Later he killed this soldier who had seen him in a church or in a labor temple having sexual intercourse, if you please, with his mother. That was the type of play that was put on. I'm so nervous.

CRICKSHAW

You're doing great. Did that really happen?

HUFFMAN

What?

CRICKSHAW

In the play. He had intercourse with his mother?

HUFFMAN

Not on stage. But they talked about it.

CRICKSHAW

That's something.

A worried FTP staff—played by Brenda Pressley, Stephen Spinella, and Brian Brophy—react to the brewing trouble with Congress. The colored pegs on the map behind them represent units of the Federal Theatre Project across the country.

In the opening scenes of Tim Robbins's *Cradle Will Rock,* Olive Stanton (Emily Watson) wakes up in a movie theatre as a newsreel flickers on the screen and a blaring voice-over narrates a bewildering string of world events. Jobless and desperate for food and shelter, Olive remains oblivious to the "big picture." Later, when she finds work as a stagehand in the Welles-Houseman production of *Faustus,* her future lover, actor John Adair (Jamey Sheridan), is astonished that she has no opinion on the Spanish Civil War.

John Adair (Jamey Sheridan), the union representative for Project 891, discusses the "big picture" with the apolitical Olive Stanton.

"Did you just crawl out from under a rock? I'm just kidding. A lot of people don't know. Spain is being attacked by Fascists from Italy, and Nazis from Germany. Roosevelt isn't doing anything 'cause he thinks the Spanish are with Russia."

Even as Blitzstein's *Cradle* was being rehearsed, Nazi dive bombers—part of a force of 175,000 troops sent by Hitler and Mussolini to support Franco's uprising—were pulverizing the defenseless Basque town of Guernica. Though the town was utterly destroyed, Guernica's memory lives on in Pablo Picasso's masterpiece of the same name, first unveiled before stunned viewers at the 1937 Paris World's Fair.

Convinced that the survival of democracy in Spain was the last bulwark against Fascism in Europe, several thousand Americans shipped off with the Abraham Lincoln Brigade, joining an international mix of volunteers. Though ill-equipped and virtually untrained, the Americans fought with extraordinary courage; fully half of them died on the battlefield defending the Spanish republic. The war also drew American writers to record the heroic and tragically lost "good fight," among them Dorothy Parker, Ernest Hemingway, Lillian Hellman, John Dos Passos, Josephine Herbst, and Upton Sinclair.

The Italian annexation of Ethiopia, act one of Mussolini's bid for a new Roman Empire, was the subject of another newsclip in *Cradle Will Rock*'s opening scene. While Il Duce's son-in-law rapturously described the beauty of bombs "opening like red blossoms," Ethiopia's emperor Haile Selassie warned the League of Nations that "it is us today. It will be you tomorrow."

Nor was Selassie wrong. Inexorably, the twentieth century was sliding into a second global conflict that would leave tens of millions dead. But despite abundant warning signs, many political and business leaders either appeased or actively colluded with the fast-growing German, Italian, and Japanese war machines. Indeed, although a European summit conference at the French Alpine resort of Évian-les-Bains predicted no threat to Jews from the rise of Nazism, Hitler was already dress-rehearsing the Holocaust. Stripping Jews of their civil rights via the infamous Nuremberg Laws, the Nazis also cracked down on Gypsies, religious Democrats, Socialists, and other political rivals. German law now demanded that Jews—already barred from work in trade or industry—identify themselves by wearing yellow six-pointed Star of David armbands.

In July 1937, one month after the triumphant New York premiere of *The Cradle Will Rock,* the gates of Buchenwald concentration camp closed on the first contingent of an eventual quarter million prisoners. A world apart, yet only a few miles away in Weimar, young Germans, like their American counterparts, were still lindying to the sounds of Benny Goodman and Fats Waller. And refreshing themselves with Coca-Cola.

Though dancing to jazz music was now officially forbidden—created as it was by artists the Nazis considered racially "subhuman"—drinking Coke was perfectly on the up-and-up. In the years just prior to World War II, the Atlanta-based beverage manufacturer—hardly alone among American companies seeking to expand their markets abroad—had opened up scores of new bottling plants in Germany, all with der Führer's blessing.

Soon, sandwiched between newsreel clips of gyrating Brazilians introducing the new samba dance craze, and Seabiscuit winning by a nose at Pimlico, American moviegoers would see the launch of Hitler's "final solution to the Jewish Question": the shattered shop windows and torched synagogues of *Kristallnacht.*

The Big Picture

HUFFMAN
Do you think I'll be called? I have so much to say.

CRICKSHAW
If they don't call you, they're crazy.

HUFFMAN
OK. It's your turn.

INT. FEDERAL THEATRE OFFICE/HALLIE'S OFFICE. DAY.
Rose reads from a newspaper as Hallie and De Rohan listen.

ROSE
"Many children now unschooled in the techniques of revolution now have an opportunity at government expense to improve their tender minds. Mother Goose is no longer a rhymed escapist. She has been studying Marx. Jack and Jill lead the class revolution."

HALLIE
What? *(she laughs)*

Now De Rohan reads.

DE ROHAN
Saturday Evening Post. The gist of it is the Federal Theatre is teaching poor people to hate and possibly murder rich children.

ROSE
This is ridiculous.

HALLIE
I am stunned. It's so absurd it's funny. *Beavers* is a fairy tale.

DE ROHAN
What about the guns, Hallie?

HALLIE
They don't shoot the big fat beaver. They just kick him out of Beaverland. So what does that say?

DE ROHAN
Class war.

HALLIE
It's a fairy tale.

DE ROHAN
The big fat beaver is a big fat capitalist.

HALLIE
The big fat beaver is a bad big fat beaver. He's a greedy beaver. He's a bad beaver.

INT. SILVANO APARTMENT. DAY.
Three children including Joey perform a song in Italian for the adults. Applause.

SILVANO
Why is he singing this song? Who taught him this song?

MAMA
I don't know.

SILVANO
Who taught him this song?

PAPA
Who? What song?

SOPHIE
His cousins. What's the problem?

SILVANO
He's singing a Blackshirt song. In my house.

MAMA
He's singing a song of Italy. He's proud to sing this song.

SILVANO
Proud. It's a Fascist song.

UNCLE
. . . It's a beautiful song.

SILVANO
Did you teach him this?

UNCLE
What if I did?

SILVANO
Where do you live?

UNCLE
Where do I live? What are you talking about?

SILVANO
This is America, you dumb shit. You want to wave your arms around, go back to Italy.

UNCLE
You insult Italy. You betray the land that gave your mother life. You spit on Italy. You slap your mother on the face.

PAPA
You spit on your mother?

He hits Silvano.

SILVANO (cont'd)

Papa, that's enough. I'm thirty-six years old. You can't smack me anymore.

Uncle smacks him.

SILVANO (cont'd)

Out. Get out.

UNCLE

What?

SILVANO

Get out of my house.

MAMA

Listen to him.

PAPA

You respect your family.

Below: Aldo Silvano's family responds to children performing a Fascist song (left). "My father came here from Italy when he was six years old," says actor John Turturro. "He knew all those Fascist songs. And yet he fought in World War II for the United States, was killed in the invasion of Normandy. I helped Tim build the character of Aldo Silvano based on him. Back then, you could be pro-Italian and pro-American at the same time, even though they fought against each other. It was complicated."

SILVANO

I respect my family. I just want him to leave.

PAPA

He's your family.

SILVANO

You can go, too.

PAPA

I can go, too. You're kicking me out, big boy. You can't afford to kick us out. Who do you think pays for this apartment?

SILVANO

Then we'll go. It costs too much to hear my son sing Fascist songs. Get the kids.

SOPHIE

Aldo, don't be crazy.

UNCLE

You call yourself an artist. The Italians were bringing art and culture to this world while your Anglo-Saxon wife's relatives were still picking fleas off of each other, living in caves.

SOPHIE

I'll get the kids.

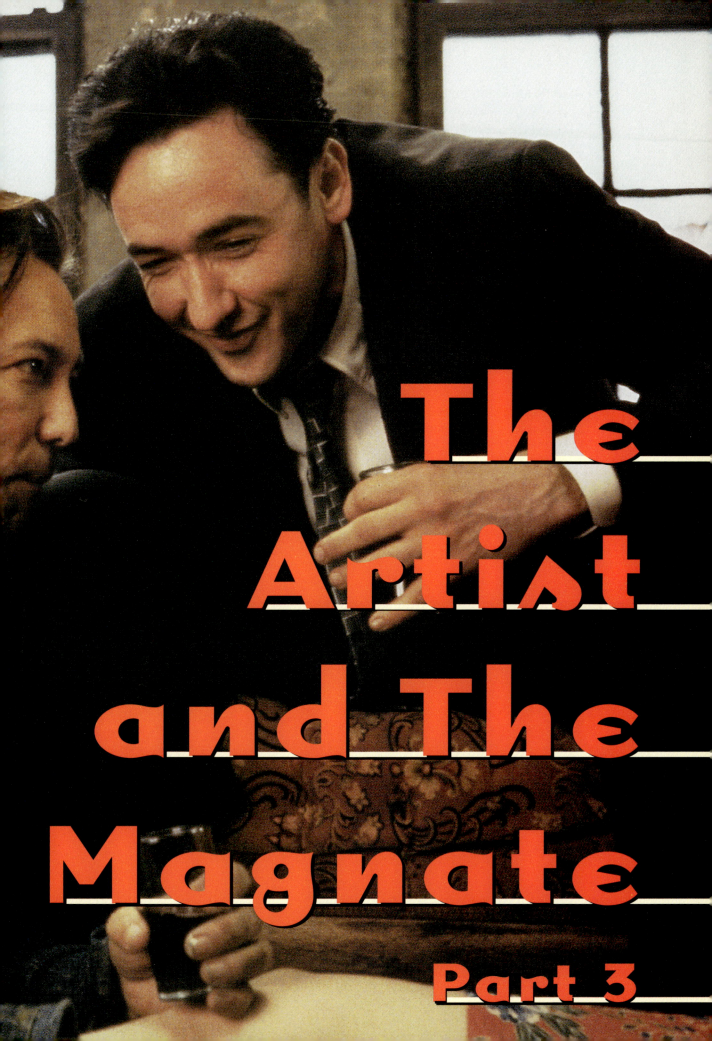

The Artist and The Magnate

Part 3

INT. VAUDEVILLE THEATRE DRESSING ROOM. DAY.
*Crickshaw is now behind the table. Hazel is the
Congressman.*

CRICKSHAW
He came to work one day, and there was a girl
there who had been a chambermaid at his hotel,
and had talked Communism to him on many
occasions. He said, "What on earth are you doing
here?" She said, "I am an actress." He said, "An
actress? Why, I know you; you are a chambermaid
in such and such a hotel." She tossed her head,
and said, "Well, it was a theatrical hotel." And
that was the point.

His joke doesn't go over. Hazel looks upset.

HUFFMAN
You're going to say that to the Congressman?

CRICKSHAW
The point I'm making is she's a maid but now
she's an actress because of her connections to
the Communists in charge.

HUFFMAN
Mr. Crickshaw, your lurid stories about chamber-
maids—this is the U.S. Congress, not a beer hall.

CRICKSHAW
I'm sorry Hazel to disappoint you. It is the furthest
thing from my intentions.

*Crickshaw moves closer. She backs away toward a
clothing rack.*

HUFFMAN
Mr. Crickshaw, there is an evil that must be
rooted out. We must choose our words carefully
or the press will mock our accusations.

CRICKSHAW *(cont'd)*
Hazel, I am attracted to you.

Pause. A gasp.

HUFFMAN
I'm afraid you are mistaken, Mr. Crickshaw.
I view our relationship in a professional way.
We are chums, nothing more.

She goes to the door and opens it.

INT. ROCKEFELLER CENTER LOBBY. DAY.
Margherita Sarfatti enters the lobby.

SARFATTI
Diego Rivera.

RIVERA
Who is that?

*The stylish Margherita Sarfatti (Susan Sarandon), a former mis-
tress of Mussolini, greets her admirers. The butler, played by
Broadway actor William Duell, appeared in the original American
production of Brecht's* Threepenny Opera, *starring Lotte Lenya.*

SARFATTI
Margherita.

RIVERA
Who?

SARFATTI
Sarfatti. How many Margheritas do you know, Diego?

RIVERA
I used to know someone by that name. A Jew.
Then she started going to bed with Fascists so I
assumed she changed her name.

SARFATTI
Fascist. Just one.

RIVERA
What?

SARFATTI
I had one Fascist. And Mussolini and I are over.

RIVERA
But you still work for him.

SARFATTI
Yes. And you are working for that cute little
Rockefeller. Times change, don't they?

RIVERA
So many roads we travel. I was wondering when
you would come.

SARFATTI
It's so big. Are you getting paid by the foot?

Rivera laughs.

SARFATTI (cont'd)
That cute little Rockefeller is hoping it will be
cheerful.

RIVERA
He sent you here to tell me this?

SARFATTI
He's worried. Whose head has fallen?

RIVERA
The head of Fascism. Hitler and your friend, the
buffoon Mussolini.

SARFATTI
My friend the buffoon loves your art. Even though
he hates your politics. Funny what he said to me.

RIVERA
And what is that?

SARFATTI
That if you are ever in trouble and you need help,
that Italy is always there for you.

Rivera laughs.

RIVERA
Oh, that's nice. But I think Mussolini will need to
hide before I do. Him and his friend Hitler.

SARFATTI
Hitler is not the friend of Mussolini.

RIVERA
You're dancing with dangerous boys, Margherita.

SARFATTI
Mussolini is a friend of many Jews.

RIVERA
How endearing. Fascist love. It's beautiful. And
you, you're not just in love. You are the publicity
queen of the new Roman Empire, writing your
articles for Hearst, selling this murderer's philoso-
phy, trying to put a human face on his Fascism.
You are at the mercy of a very powerful man.

SARFATTI
As are we all, Diego. As are we all.

INT. MATHERS'S MANSION (PARLOR). NIGHT.
*We see the Countess in a sitting room with Gray Mathers
and Carlo, who is singing a terrible aria. Mathers crosses
to the radio, turning it on, loudly. The Countess crosses to
the radio and turns it off.*

MATHERS
For God's sake, it's the only thing that makes this
singing bearable.

COUNTESS
Have an open mind, dear.

MATHERS
What is he singing about, anyway?

COUNTESS
I'm not sure. I think it has something to do with
the woes of a cobbler.

MATHERS
A cobbler?

COUNTESS
A shoemaker.

MATHERS
Ridiculous.

Benito Mussolini's Italian version of Fascism ran for several years before its German and Spanish interpretations under Hitler and Franco moved it closer to conquering the world political stage.

The word *fascism* comes from *fascio*, Italian for "bundle," in turn derived from the Latin *fasces*—a cluster of birch or elm rods wound with a red strap and with an axe blade protruding from the top end. In ancient Rome, the fasces were carried in procession before the magistrates and represented the authority of law and the state's authority to punish criminals by execution. They made a fitting emblem for Mussolini's Fascist Party as it embarked on its quest to restore the glories of the Roman Empire. In the United States, the fasces became popular as a heroic architectural ornament and can still be seen decorating the entrances of many WPA-era government buildings.

Fascism itself is an aggressively nationalistic, often racially supremacist, political system that subordinates individual rights to the totalitarian power of the state. Fascist governments do not collectivize property as under Communism; instead, the state and industry enter into a strategic partnership that regulates economic activity but leaves ownership of big businesses in private hands.

Ironically, Mussolini began his political career as a Socialist. He even edited the party newspaper *Avanti!* ("Forward!"), but after World War I his disillusionment with the Bolshevik Revolution pushed him increasingly toward the right. Beginning in 1919, Italy was convulsed by a wave of strikes that culminated in the occupation of whole factories by workers in the cities of the industrial north. In the countryside, peasants seized estates and refused to pay rents. Mussolini organized a counterforce of students and ex-soldiers into paramilitary units known as the Blackshirts. Blackshirt squads attacked the offices of radical organizations and newspapers, and engaged in bloody street fights with leftist demonstrators and strikers. Soon, frightened industrialists and landlords were pouring economic support into Mussolini's new Partito Nazionale Fascista, which won a parliamentary majority in the elections of 1924. A year later, Mussolini took on permanent dictatorial powers as supreme leader, or "Il Duce." Within a few years, universal suffrage was abolished, and Italy was reduced to a centralized, single-party police state.

Fascism for Sale

One of the most complex characters in Tim Robbins's *Cradle Will Rock* is the charming and cultivated Margherita Sarfatti (Susan Sarandon), Mussolini's ex-mistress and his cultural emissary to the United States. The film depicts her delivering Italian Renaissance masterpieces to the fictional philistine industrialist and art collector Gray Mathers in exchange for steel to build Il Duce's war machine.

Born Jewish, Sarfatti converted to Catholicism and maintained an apparently unshakable faith in the virtues of Mussolini's regime. Part of Sarfatti's mission was to sell Italian Fascism abroad, and in William Randolph Hearst (John Carpenter) she found an able and willing collaborator. Hearst's vast newspaper network allowed Sarfatti to write articles that made totalitarianism sound downright nurturing: "Fascism from a political viewpoint does not regard the citizen as an individual or cell detached from the great bosom of the state and nation."

Nor was the appeal of the Italian brand of Fascism entirely lost on the United States. Its silencing of the left and mobilization of industry were seen as important plusses by Depression-scarred lower middle classes and

Mussolini looks over Nazi troops with his German counterpart, Adolf Hitler, during Il Duce's state visit to Munich in September 1937.

capitalists alike. Many pro-Roosevelt business leaders, including the president of the Bank of America, openly admired Mussolini's economic policies, as did New Deal planners who balked only at Il Duce's brutal military adventures and extreme nationalism. The powerful Wall Street securities broker Julius A. Basche went so far as to declare him a "man every country needs," since "autocracy is the only solution to the world's problems."

Today such statements may strike us as, well, fascist. Yet to some at the time Sarfatti's description of women's place within Il Duce's system may have sounded like a comforting return to "traditional" family values. "Women inscribed in the Fascist party are encouraged to give their entire attention to the care of maternity and infancy," she wrote in Hearst's *Herald Tribune*. "It may be said that Fascism itself adopts and aims at the divine, unassuming, generous Christian virtue of charity."

COUNTESS
I would appreciate it if you wouldn't cast aspersions so loudly in front of my protégé.

MATHERS
Protégé?

COUNTESS
I certainly kept my mouth shut at lunch today. I don't interfere with your affairs.

MATHERS
You wouldn't understand them.

COUNTESS
I most certainly do understand them. You are doing business with Benito Mussolini, who is a dangerous man in my estimation.

MATHERS
In your estimation.

COUNTESS
I am looking beyond your profit margin to a moral place, dear. A terribly complex place we all have to deal with in the coming years. We have Jewish friends, you know.

Carlo continues moaning.

INT. MAXINE ELLIOTT'S THEATRE. NIGHT.
Auditions have begun. Canada and Dulce sing. Silvano and family enter, bundled up, carrying suitcases. Blitzstein, Houseman and Welles watch from the house. In the wings we see:

OLIVE
But I haven't gotten official permission.

ADAIR
Just go up there; don't say anything, don't apologize, just sing from your heart.

Olive Stanton approaches the piano in the middle of the stage. She begins to sing.

OLIVE
I'M CHECKING HOME NOW,
CALL IT A NIGHT.

GOIN' UP TO MY ROOM,
TURN ON THE LIGHT.
JESUS, TURN OFF THAT LIGHT.

We see Welles sitting with Blitzstein and Houseman in the audience.

WELLES
This is the look of the prostitute. Fresh, innocent,

Hazel Huffman (Joan Cusack) testifying before the Dies Committee. "What drives her to Washington," explains Cusack, "is a belief that the Communistic influence in the Federal Theatre is ruining the project, turning it into an anti-Fascist cesspool. And she has a lot of examples."

skinny. I don't want some brassy, pulchritudinous whore, Jack. I want some gal driven to sell her body because she's hungry. The Market Crash of '29 made whores of many gals. You'd find that out if you were heterosexual, Jack.

OLIVE
FOR TWO DAYS OUT OF SEVEN
TWO DOLLAR BILLS I'M GIVEN.

Title: FIVE MONTHS LATER, SUMMER 1937

OLIVE
SO I'M JUST SEARCHING ALONG THE STREET,
FOR ON THOSE FIVE DAYS IT'S NICE TO EAT.
JESUS, JESUS, WHO SAID LET'S EAT?

WELLES
Why did we cast her? She's terrible.

All of a sudden the glass set on the stage begins to rock back and forth, blinding lights shoot up from beneath the actors.

HOUSEMAN
It's your sets that are horrible. No one knows where they are. Actors are entering in fear of their lives.

WELLES
You say another word, Jack, and I'll murder you. What the fuck is going on? Someone explain to me how it is possible that the finale cues are playing in the first act. Abe! Where the fuck are you?

INT. FEDERAL THEATRE OFFICES. NIGHT.
We start on a piece of paper and pull out to reveal Flanagan, O'Hara, De Rohan, and Paul Edwards.

EDWARDS
Twenty percent.

HALLIE
That's three thousand people out of work.

EDWARDS
Effective immediately. Because of the cuts and reorganization, any new play, musical performance, or art gallery is prohibited from opening before July 1st.

HALLIE
This is an outrage.

EDWARDS
Hallie.

ROSE
Hallie, our train leaves in twenty minutes. We really must leave.

HALLIE

Paul, we'll be down in Washington for two days. Can't this wait until I return?

EDWARDS

This has gone out to all projects already. I play by the book.

HALLIE

Of course you do, Paul. But you should at least give me the chance to deal with the directors personally. Good Lord, *Cradle Will Rock* opens tomorrow. Does this mean the opening is canceled?

EDWARDS

I'm afraid so.

HALLIE

That's just downright disgraceful behavior. Rose, get me Jack Houseman on the phone. Urgent.

O'HARA

Hallie, our train is the last one to Washington this evening. If we miss the train you will be unable to appear in front of the Committee. I must insist that we leave.

EDWARDS

I'll call Mr. Houseman and explain everything.

They exit.

During the late 1930s, *while the Roosevelt administration pursued its policy of official neutrality, some American businesses were finding a profitable niche within the growing Fascist war machines of Germany and Italy. The economic and ideological embrace of Hitler and Mussolini by America's corporate titans is made clear in the following excerpt from historian Michael Parenti's* Blackshirts and Reds: Rational Fascism and the Overthrow of Communism:

Italian Fascism and German Nazism had their admirers within the U.S. business community and the corporate-owned press. Bankers, publishers, and industrialists, including the likes of Henry Ford, traveled to Rome and Berlin to pay homage, receive medals, and strike profitable deals. Many did their utmost to advance the Nazi war effort, sharing military-industrial secrets and engaging in secret transactions with the Nazi government, even after the United States entered the war.* During the 1920s and early 1930s, major publications like *Fortune,* the *Wall Street Journal, Saturday Evening Post, New York Times, Chicago Tribune,* and *Christian Science Monitor* hailed Mussolini as the man who rescued Italy from anarchy and radicalism....

The Italian-language press in the United States eagerly joined the chorus. The two most influential newspapers, *L'Italia* of San Francisco, financed largely by A.P. Giannini's Bank of America, and *Il Progresso* of New York, owned by multimillionaire Generoso Pope, looked favorably on the fascist regime and suggested that the United States could benefit from a similar social order.

Some dissenters refused to join the "We Adore Benito" chorus. *The Nation* reminded its readers that Mussolini was not saving democracy but destroying it. Progressives of all stripes and various labor leaders denounced fascism. But their critical sentiments received little exposure in the U.S. corporate media.

As with Mussolini, so with Hitler. The press did not look too unkindly upon *der Fuehrer's* Nazi dictatorship. There was a strong "Give Adolph a Chance" contingent, some of it greased by Nazi money. In exchange for more positive coverage in the Hearst newspapers, for instance, the Nazis paid almost ten times the standard subscription rate for Hearst's INS wire service. In return, William

Randolph Hearst instructed his correspondents in Germany to file friendly reports about Hitler's regime. Those who refused were transferred or fired. Hearst newspapers even opened their pages to occasional guest columns by prominent Nazi leaders like Alfred Rosenberg and Hermann Göring.

By the mid to late 1930s, Italy and Germany, allied with Japan, another industrial latecomer, were aggressively seeking a share of the world's markets and colonial booty, an expansionism that brought them increasingly into conflict with more established Western capitalist nations like Great Britain, France, and the United States. As the clouds of war gathered, U.S. press opinion about the Axis powers took on a decisively critical tone....

What happened to the U.S. businesses that collaborated with fascism? The Rockefeller family's Chase National Bank used its Paris office in Vichy France to help launder German money to facilitate Nazi international trade during the war, and did so with complete impunity. Corporations like DuPont, Ford, General Motors, and ITT owned factories in enemy countries that produced fuel, tanks, and planes that wreaked havoc on Allied forces. After the war, instead of being prosecuted for treason, ITT collected $27 million from the U.S. government for war damages inflicted on its German plants by Allied bombings. General Motors collected over $33 million. Pilots were given instructions not to hit factories in Germany that were owned by U.S. firms. Thus Cologne was almost leveled by Allied bombing but its Ford plant, providing military equipment for the Nazi army, was untouched; indeed, German civilians began using the plant as an air raid shelter.*

* Charles Higham, *Trading with the Enemy* (New York: Dell, 1983).

Kudos for Adolf & Benito

INT. CONGRESSIONAL CHAMBER. NIGHT.

Huffman has gotten her wish. She testifies before the Dies Committee on Un-American Activities. A panel of Congressmen listen patiently as Huffman lays it on.

HUFFMAN
I can conclude by saying that I thank you for your patience and your kindness to me. We certainly hope that the results of this committee will be to clear out the Communism on the Federal Project, and the pro-Communism, and place the project in the hands of efficient professional people.

CHAIRMAN DIES
Place it in the hands of people who are in sympathy with the American home and government; is that what you mean?

HUFFMAN
I'm sorry, Mr. Chairman. I'm not sure what you mean.

INT. VAUDEVILLE THEATRE DRESSING ROOM. NIGHT.

Crickshaw listens to Huffman's testimony on the radio. He is very drunk.

CHAIRMAN DIES (V.O.)
I mean, you hope it will be placed in the hands of those who are opposed to Communism? Is that what you mean?

HUFFMAN (V.O.)
Yes. That is what I mean.

CHAIRMAN DIES (V.O.)
Thank you very much for coming before this committee and giving us the facts that you have.

HUFFMAN (V.O.)
Well, thank you for having this committee and receiving the facts that I have.

There is a pounding on the door.

STAGE MANAGER (V.O.)
Mr. Crickshaw, you're on.

CRICKSHAW
She loves you, she loves you not.

INT. MAXINE ELLIOTT'S THEATRE. NIGHT.

LARRY (SILVANO)
Open shop is when a worker can be kicked around, demoted, fired, just like that—he's all alone. He's free—free to be wiped out. Closed shop. He's got fifty thousand other workers with him ready to back him up, every one of them to

the last lunch pail. The difference. This is an open shop.

He holds up his hands, fingers spread wide.

LARRY (SILVANO)
This is a closed shop.

He holds up a fist.

LARRY (SILVANO)
This is a union.

ADAIR
Order in the courtroom! Next case, Reverend Salvation!

STAGE MANAGER
The Liberty Committee! The Liberty Committee!

HOUSEMAN
Where are they?

VOICES
We're coming. We're ready.

STAGE MANAGER
Stand by.

WELLES
Abe, what is the cue number?

Pause.

WELLES
Abe!

FEDER
Yes!

WELLES
Where would you like to go from?

FEDER
Cue 15.

STAGE MANAGER
Cue 15. Moll's line: "Reverend Salvation. Habitual prostitute since 1915."

OLIVE
Reverend Salvation. Habitual.

STAGE MANAGER
Wait!

HOUSEMAN
When they say go, dear.

OLIVE
I've never done this before.

WELLES

I'm astonished.

STAGE MANAGER

Ready, Abe?

FEDER

Ready.

STAGE MANAGER

Go cue.

Pause.

HOUSEMAN

That's you.

OLIVE

Me?

HOUSEMAN

Yes, you.

OLIVE

What do I do?

WELLES

Say the fucking line.

If *The Cradle Will Rock* was to achieve its maximum dramatic punch, Welles and Houseman knew they would have to populate Blitzstein's Steeltown with an absolutely credible cast. Even though they drew mainly from the wide variety of relief-work talent within the WPA, they also brought in established actors Will Geer to play Mr. Mister and Howard da Silva to portray his incorruptible antagonist Larry Foreman.

In the movie, Robbins zeroes in on the dramatic moment when John Adair practically pushes Olive Stanton on stage to audition for the role of Moll. Vulnerable and awkward, Stanton captivates Welles, who declares, "This is the look of the prostitute. Fresh, innocent, skinny. I don't want some brassy, pulchritudinous whore, Jack. I want some gal driven to sell her body because she's hungry."

In casting to authenticate the *Cradle* days of 1937, Robbins went on something of a casting spree from contemporary Broadway. Erin Hill, who plays Sandra Mescal, came from *Cabaret*. Tim Jerome went on hiatus from *Beauty and the Beast* to play Bert Weston. Victoria Clark and Henry Stram jumped ship from *Titanic* to take on roles as Dulce Fox and Hiram Sherman. Tony winner Audra McDonald took an afternoon off from *Ragtime* to sing Marc Blitzstein's "Joe Worker" live in Madison Square Park amid a simulated swirl of mounted police and fleeing protesters.

Robbins also drew on his own version of Project 891: the Actor's Gang, a critically acclaimed theatre ensemble

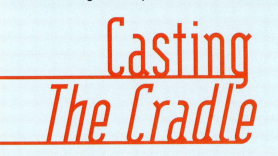

Casting
The Cradle

founded in 1981 by Robbins and his friends at UCLA. The Actor's Gang was known for staging aggressive and fearless theater, their subjects taken from real-life events hot off the press in a style reminiscent of the FTP's Living Newspapers.

Eight "gang" members made the pilgrimage to New York to help rock Robbins's *Cradle*: Susan Heimbinder as Blitzstein's wife, Eva; Lee Arenberg, who plays Abe "Lightning" Feder; Ned Bellamy as WPA administrator Paul Edwards; V. J. Foster as Gray Mathers's chauffeur; and Kyle Gass and Jack Black as the gay vaudeville trainees ("We're not Red, darling. Pink. Like a flower.") who drive Tommy Crickshaw (Bill Murray) over the edge. Gang members Patti Tippo and Mike Rivkin also joined the cast.

Robbins knew exactly what he was looking for when he cast the lead roles but still requested auditions. Emily Watson says that when the time came to sing for the director she was as nervous as Olive Stanton must have been that first night at the Venice Theatre when Feder swiveled his spotlight to catch her rising up out of the audience, and Blitzstein, alone on stage at the piano, laid down the accompaniment to "Moll's Song."

Above: Blitzstein (center) rehearses song numbers with the cast from Cradle. *Center: Olive Stanton, around 1937.*

OLIVE (MOLL)
Reverend Salvation. Habitual prostitute since 1915.

The lights change. The Liberty Committee enters. Marvel enters saying the wrong line. Someone trips. The Steeltown sign falls, breaking a glass tower. Chaos.

ADAIR
Break time. Call it a night.

We see Welles, about to blow.

INT. VAUDEVILLE THEATRE BACKSTAGE. NIGHT.

Crickshaw stumbles, dummy in hand. The two unfunny comedians, Sid and Larry, are on stage performing Crickshaw's act. One is a dummy.

CRICKSHAW
What's going on?

STAGE MANAGER
There you are, Mr. Crickshaw. I pounded on your door. I didn't hear an answer.

CRICKSHAW
Am I on next?

STAGE MANAGER
No, sir. This is your slot. I sent Sid and Larry out to cover for you.

CRICKSHAW
That's my act.

STAGE MANAGER
I'm sorry, sir. We had to do something.

INT. ROCKEFELLER CENTER LOBBY. NIGHT.

The mural is fully fleshed out, nearly finished. Nelson Rockefeller, Aide, and a lawyer, address Diego. On the mural behind Diego we see the face of Vladimir Lenin.

AIDE
Why can't you paint another face over it?

DIEGO
Would you prefer Stalin? I don't. I was kicked out of the party for disagreeing with him; but if you want I'll paint Stalin.

LAWYER
You're not being cooperative.

A furious Nelson Rockefeller (John Cusack, below) confronts Diego Rivera (Ruben Blades, above right) when he discovers that the mural features the face of Vladimir Lenin. "Knowing Rivera's background," says Blades, "Rockefeller should have seen this coming. People should have said to him, 'You're hiring a Communist to paint a mural in Rockefeller Center, what do you think he's gonna paint—Snow White?'"

DIEGO

I am so. I told you I would paint Abraham Lincoln on the other side surrounded by freed slaves to counterbalance Lenin. You rejected that idea.

AIDE

Why Lenin?

DIEGO

He's a revolutionary leader. Like your Jefferson or Washington.

ROCKEFELLER

There's an idea. How about Jefferson?

AIDE

That's not a bad idea. What do you say, Diego?

DIEGO

Ridiculous. I said Lincoln to balance the other side but Lenin stays.

ROCKEFELLER

This is not our revolution. This is the United States, not Russia.

DIEGO

I am Diego Rivera, not Frederic Remington.

AIDE

You understand that it is entirely inappropriate to have a Communist leader featured in the lobby of a Rockefeller building.

DIEGO

I believe that nothing in art is inappropriate. I paint what I see.

LAWYER

We're going to have to insist that the face be removed.

DIEGO

Absolutely not!

ROCKEFELLER

Look, you son of a bitch. We're trying to be nice. This is a betrayal.

RIVERA

A betrayal?

ROCKEFELLER

There was no indication in your sketches that you would be featuring Communist leaders in the mural. When you were hired you were hired on the basis of your sketches. You've changed it. It's not fair.

DIEGO

Lenin stays!

Rockefeller exits with lackeys.

INT. MAXINE ELLIOTT'S THEATRE (STAGE). NIGHT.

WELLES

How the hell will we open without a cue-to-cue?

HOUSEMAN

The cast is called early. We'll cue-to-cue in the morning.

WELLES

There are 175 cues to go.

HOUSEMAN

Perhaps if you cut some of the cues like a good little boy we'd be able to finish.

AUGUSTA

Jack, there's a call from Hallie Flanagan's office.

HOUSEMAN

Not now, Augusta, I'm in the middle of an argument.

INT. MAXINE ELLIOTT'S THEATRE (BASEMENT). NIGHT.

We follow Augusta. Sandra is pregnant. Olive is crying, being comforted by Dulce and Canada. John Adair comes by.

DULCE

He didn't mean it. He's very tense.

CANADA

This always happens in cue-to-cues.

ADAIR

Union rules say we have a break until twelve noon. I'll be here at twelve noon. Olive! Let's go—

We follow Augusta into a room.

The Battle for Rockefeller Center

The clash between Mexican muralist Diego Rivera and his patron Nelson Rockefeller occurred in the early thirties, but by weaving it into the events of 1937, Tim Robbins brings out all the more vividly the artistic and social conflicts that culminated in the *Cradle* moment.

Born in 1886 and trained in the workshop of great folk artist José Guadalupe Posada, Rivera refused to settle into the prevailing European mode that produced paintings of ecstatic virgins, delectable Cupids, portraits of grand personages, and sculptures with titles like *Après L'Orgie*. Instead, he reached deep into his country's Indian and mestizo traditions for inspiration, determined "to make the people the hero of mural painting." As a young man he worked to the rhythms of the Mexican Revolution, spending sixteen-hour days perched on scaffolds, creating popular murals with a pistol at his waist. "To set a line for the critics," he said. By the mid-1920s, the power of Rivera's work had gained him international recognition.

Enter a young Nelson Rockefeller, armed with a $21,000 commission to paint a mural in the lobby of Rockefeller Center's soaring RCA Building. Rebuffed by Matisse and Picasso, Rockefeller was bent on securing Rivera's services, not least because the painter was a favorite of his mother, Abby Aldrich, later a founder of the Museum of Modern Art.

Rockefeller, who later served as New York State governor and vice president under Gerald Ford, had grown up with an understanding of art and power worlds apart from that of his chosen muralist. Rockefeller's grandfather, the original John D., epitomized the top-hatted monopolist and was one of the wealthiest and most hated men in the world. Born in 1908, Nelson was six when his father, John D., Jr., ordered company guards to break the strike at the family's Ludlow, Colorado, mining operation at all costs. In multiple armed assaults, dozens of miners, their wives, and children were killed or wounded.

Yet Nelson longed to adorn the walls of his family's new icon of corporate power with populist images of heroic toil and triumph—so much so that he ignored Rivera's avowed Marxism. Nelson went so far as to defend Rivera's right to free expression in a battle over a "Communist" tableau created in Detroit for Henry Ford's son Edsel. He enthusiastically approved the artist's sketches for the RCA Building lobby in November 1932.

The following May, in the midst of his frenzied rendering of the Rockefeller mural, Rivera was interviewed at the work site by a reporter who noted his depiction of Vladimir Ilyich Lenin, the Soviet leader, clasping hands with a black American sharecropper, a Russian soldier, and an "international" industrial worker. When the *World-Telegram* hit the streets blaring the headline "Rivera Paints Scenes of Communist Activity and John D., Jr., Foots the Bill," Nelson was forced to act.

"Viewing the progress of your thrilling mural," he wrote Rivera in a letter, "I noticed that in the most recent portion of the painting you had included a portrait of Lenin. The piece is beautifully painted but might seriously offend a great many people. As much as I dislike to do so, I am afraid we must ask you to substitute the face of some unknown man where Lenin's face now appears."

Insisting that Lenin's figure had appeared in even his earliest sketches, Rivera refused to eradicate the portrait and, little imagining that he would be taken literally, asserted that he would sooner see his work destroyed than mutilated. In an atmosphere of escalating acrimony, Nelson barred Rivera, had his guards secure the lobby, and ordered the mural screened from view. When demonstrators gathered outside to protest what Rivera called "an act of cultural vandalism," they were clubbed down by mounted police.

Early in 1934, the nearly completed fresco, *Man at the*

Left and below: The Mexican painter Diego Rivera, early 1930s.

Crossroads Looking with Hope and High Vision to the Choosing of a New and Better Future, was jackhammered off the wall and replaced with the politically uncontroversial *American Progress,* by José Luis Sert.

Fortunately, one of Rivera's assistants, the painter Lucienne Bloch, had documented the ill-fated mural and was later able to "reconstruct" it in the Palacio de Bellas Artes in Mexico City, with one significant addition: "a portrait of John D. Rockefeller, Jr., inserted into the nightclub scene, his head but a short distance away from the venereal disease germs pictured in the microscope."

It is worth noting that on his rollercoaster expedition to New York City, Rivera was accompanied by his wife, Frida Kahlo. Kahlo's prolific outpouring of small-scale canvases stands as an extraordinary counterpoint to Rivera's heroically scaled compositions. In the years since her death in 1954, appreciation for Kahlo's vibrant, luminously personal self-portraits has grown steadily, and today she ranks as one of the century's most respected and influential artists.

AUGUSTA
He can't come to the phone right now.

HIRAM
Augusta, how the hell are we supposed to get there in total darkness?

AUGUSTA
I'll have him call.

She hangs up.

AUGUSTA (*cont'd*)
I am so sorry. I should get a torch. Abe, do you have a flashlight?

FEDER
Light a match.

HOUSEMAN
Is it really fucking necessary to have eight lighting cues for one entrance?

WELLES
It's an important entrance. Who's the fucking director? I'm the director.

HOUSEMAN
Yes, of a fucking disaster.

WELLES
A disaster like your *Hamlet,* Jack.

SILVANO
I have to take my kids to a free clinic. Tell Mr. Welles I'll be in at 11:30.

HOUSEMAN
That's it. I'm leaving.

WELLES
You can't leave, you're the producer.

HOUSEMAN
As the producer I can fire anyone I please, and I am fucking fired.

WELLES
You'll be back, you'll be crawling back like a bitch to his master, groveling after little pieces of meat.

MARVEL
I'm glad he didn't get to me. I can't remember my lines. I'm stricken with cerebral malaise.

We see Blitzstein freaking out, inconsolable, blubbering.

INT. MATHERS'S MANSION (PARLOR). NIGHT.
Gray Mathers stands dressed in a ridiculous eighteenth-century French royalty costume complete with a long-haired

wig and platform shoes. A tailor attends to the hem of the waistcoat. Mathers is on the phone.

MATHERS

First he kills my deals with Italy. Now he's telling me how to run my business. I'm not budging. Well, let him call, the crippled son of a bitch. Let him call.

He hangs up. The Countess, dressed as Marie Antoinette, dances by with Carlo.

MATHERS

Jimminy Jesus. The bastards. Get this goddamned thing off of me. Roosevelt's going to call.

COUNTESS

It looks good. You look adorable.

MATHERS

I don't want to look adorable. I want to look angry.

COUNTESS

We'll make a stunning pair.

TAILOR

I need to let it out.

COUNTESS

Will it be ready for tomorrow?

TAILOR

Oui, madam.

Previous page: Production designer Richard Hoover chose a defunct WPA-era Newark, New Jersey, bank to act as a stand-in for the Rockefeller Center lobby, circa 1934. A team of painters spent ten days re-creating the legendary Diego Rivera mural before jackhammers obliterated it once again—this time on camera. Above: In a detail from the finished mural, Rivera presages the age of television.

MATHERS

Bastard wants me to join the rest of Little Steel in acknowledging the union.

COUNTESS

Oh how terrible.

MATHERS

It is terrible.

COUNTESS

Worse than a strike.

MATHERS

Not worse than a strike.

COUNTESS

I know so little.

A beat.

COUNTESS

Oh Gray, dear. That awful woman came by. Left two packages.

MATHERS
Packages? Awful woman?

COUNTESS
Carlo, can you grab the packages?

Carlo doesn't move. The butler appears with the package.

BUTLER
Mr. Mathers, sir. A parcel was left for you by one Margherita Sarfatti.

MATHERS
Thank you, Paul.

COUNTESS
What's in it?

MATHERS
So nosy.

COUNTESS
Pray tell.

MATHERS
Perhaps it's a surprise. Suppose it were a gift?

COUNTESS
From Sarfatti?

MATHERS
Purchased through her. For you.

COUNTESS
Interesting.

MATHERS
Now mind your business.

INT. NEW SILVANO APARTMENT. NIGHT.
Silvano and Sophie lie in bed in a small apartment. The kids are on a mattress on the floor. Much harder times.

SOPHIE
Did you see the papers today?

SILVANO
No.

SOPHIE
It was like *Cradle Will Rock* was on the front page. Steel strike. Mathers' Steel.

SILVANO
Really?

SOPHIE
Same themes. Same words almost. It's a dangerous play you're in.

SILVANO
It's a great role. I'm lucky, huh?

SOPHIE
Mmmm.

SILVANO
I just don't want to blow it. It's too important.

CHANCE
Daddy, are we going to lose our room?

SILVANO
No, Chance. What makes you say that?

CHANCE
Joey told me.

JOEY
Michael O'Brien's family lost their apartment. He doesn't go to school anymore.

SILVANO
Oh. Well, Daddy's got a job so we're all right.

JOEY
Michael O'Brien's father had a job and then he lost it and then they were poor.

SILVANO
Well, we're poor but we're going to be fine. We should say some prayers just to be safe though, all right?

The Countess (Vanessa Redgrave) and Gray Mathers (Philip Baker Hall) dress up as French royalty for a masquerade ball.

JOEY
All right.

INT. ADAIR APARTMENT. NIGHT.

Olive and John Adair lie in bed. It is obvious from their behavior that they have been lovers for a few months.

OLIVE
John?

ADAIR
Yeah?

OLIVE
Am I horrible?

ADAIR
Huh?

OLIVE
In the play. Am I horrible?

ADAIR
No, you're not horrible.

A re-creation of the glass-and-chrome set that was originally planned for The Cradle Will Rock *before government officials shut down the theatre. "I think Blitzstein himself would have agreed that the crazy set Orson designed was a bad idea from the beginning," says Hank Azaria. "Even Welles knew it after a while."*

OLIVE
Am I not good?

ADAIR
No, you're good.

OLIVE
But I'm not great.

A pause.

ADAIR
You're great . . . at times.

A pause.

ADAIR
It's hard to be great. Some actors can be great all the time. This is your first role. You try hard. Listen, you're better off than you were.

INT. BLITZSTEIN APT. NIGHT.

Blitzstein and demons.

BRECHT
You suck. Your play is horrible, indulgent, masturbatory nonsense.

BLITZSTEIN
You don't really believe that?

BRECHT
You hear what you want to hear.

"Did you see the paper today?" Sophie Silvano (Barbara Sukowa) asks her husband (John Turturro) in Robbins's movie. "It was like *Cradle Will Rock* was on the front page. Steel strike.... Same themes. Same words almost. It's a dangerous play you're in."

Though Marc Blitzstein's explosive musical takes place in a mythical city called Steeltown, real-life struggles between workers and management were taking place all over the country in the thirties. Conditions for steelworkers at the time were deplorable: In 1933 the average employee made $369 a year, on which he was expected to support an average of six dependents. Occupational illnesses such as pneumonia and carbon monoxide poisoning took hundreds of lives every year. Due to shockingly outdated equipment and an almost complete lack of safety regulations, accidents were rampant. In one year alone, nearly 23,000 steelworkers were either killed, permanently disabled, or forced to stop working because of injuries.

It was no accident that theatergoers experienced an exhilarating sense of life paralleling art when witnessing the early performances of *Cradle*. Blitzstein believed that like other artists, "composers must come out into the open, they must fight the battle with other workers." And indeed the battle lines were sharply drawn, with dialogue to match.

"No tin-hat brigade of goose-stepping vigilantes or Bible-babbling mob of blackguarding corporation-scoundrels will prevent the onward march of labor," was not a line written by Blitzstein for his defiant Steeltown worker hero. It was union organizer John L. Lewis's retort to Henry Ford after the automobile magnate claimed he would "never recognize the United Auto Workers (UAW) or any other union."

Lewis, head of the fledgling Congress of Industrial Organizations (CIO), believed the only hope for workers lay in unionizing entire industries. Opposing the CIO was a formidable cast of real-life Gray Mathers, determined to break the unions and run big business their way. Henry Ford presided over a "service department" of six hundred pistol- and blackjack-toting goons. General Motors (GM), the nation's largest industrial employer, spent $1 million undermining the UAW with what a U.S. Senate committee called "the most colossal supersystem of spies yet devised in any American corporation."

Despite the campaign of intimidation, the CIO scored huge wins in the months prior to the "wildcat" premiere of *The Cradle Will Rock*. First came the successful sit-down

A striker in San Francisco, 1934.

strikes against General Motors, during which *Time* magazine commented that Detroiters were "getting an idea of what a revolution feels like." Next, steel strikers took over their plants, forcing U.S. Steel to recognize their union, concede a 10 percent wage increase, a 40-hour workweek, and time and a half for overtime.

By April, the steel union had grown to nearly 300,000 members. In the course of the year, almost 5 million workers took part in some kind of strike action—twice as many as in 1936—including a half-million who participated in sit-down strikes. At year's end, the CIO claimed 3.7 million members.

But by mid-1937, the labor battle in America's Steel-towns was turning increasingly bloody as efforts to unionize "little steel" companies, like Republic Steel with 53,000 workers, met with fierce resistance. Republic's own Mr. Mister, Tom Girdler, declared he would "rather go back to hoeing potatoes" than give in to union organizers, and on May 30, ordered the Chicago police to attack a peaceful demonstration of racially mixed workers and sympathizers. Ten people were killed and over sixty others were wounded in what came to be known as the Memorial Day Massacre. That June, as *The Cradle Will Rock* neared its audacious premiere, eight more strikers were killed and 160 seriously wounded in Cleveland, Youngstown, and Massillon. Eventually, at great cost, the unions prevailed.

Today, only six decades after their hard-won victories, American steelmaking has all but vanished. In 1995, Bethlehem Steel shut down its last H-Beam plant, effectively ending 120 years of steelmaking in the Lehigh Valley. Super-strong, wide-flange H-Beams, known as "Bethlehem Sections," had been used in scores of WPA-era projects, from the Golden Gate and George Washington Bridges to the Empire State Building.

Steeltown Is Our Town

Olive Stanton and John Adair the night before Cradle *opens. "She thinks he's this great actor and she's really impressed," says Emily Watson of her character. "This is her first job in a couple of years probably. And they are living together very quickly, so it's a home, apart from anything else."*

EVA

If you slept a little more you might have had a shot.

BRECHT

Garbage.

EVA

It's not the end of the world.

INT. NEW SILVANO APARTMENT. NIGHT.

The kids asleep now, Silvano and Sophie lie in bed, talking quietly.

SOPHIE

I saw a rat today.

SILVANO

Where?

SOPHIE

In here.

A pause.

SOPHIE *(cont'd)*

Your mama stopped by. She was kind of shocked about how we're living.

SILVANO

She would be.

SOPHIE

I think she wants to help.

SILVANO

No.

SOPHIE

We could use the money.

SILVANO

I don't want my family's money.

SOPHIE

So the kids go hungry because of your pride. Your politics.

SILVANO

You want chubby little Fascists?

SOPHIE

No, but I don't want to wait with them on soup lines. I don't want them . . .

90

SILVANO

What would that teach them, to take my parents' money? That it's alright to believe in something or have pride but if you're just a little bit hungry, sell it?

SOPHIE

There's rats in here, Aldo.

EXT. WASHINGTON D.C. MORNING.

Title: THE NEXT DAY

Hallie walks with O'Hara and De Rohan toward the Capitol Building.

O'HARA

Paul Edwards couldn't reach Jack Houseman last night. He's trying again today.

HALLIE

Keep on top of that. Tell Rose to reassure Jack that we will find a way to do his show.

They run into Harry Hopkins, who is waiting for them.

HOPKINS

They've been chomping at the bit for you. They're all acting as if they have been wanting to talk to you all along.

HALLIE

Twenty percent cuts, Harry. I had no warning.

HOPKINS

It's a temporary measure, a stop gap, a cash flow problem, a nightmare. We'll get the twenty percent back, Hallie.

HALLIE

Can I hold you to that?

HOPKINS

Yes.

DE ROHAN

Who testified last night?

HOPKINS

Hazel Huffman. A real nut case. Got good headlines, though. Most of the press is so bored with this committee, they just bite the bait and print the highlights. They're all coming back for you though, Hallie.

HALLIE

I'm honored.

HOPKINS

Not to put any pressure on you, but a good showing today will invariably help. The Congressmen will be in good shape today. None of them were out drinking last night.

EXT. MAXINE ELLIOTT'S THEATRE. DAY.

Start on chains, locks on front doors of theatre. We pan over to reveal John Houseman talking to a U.S. soldier.

SOLDIER

By order of the Federal Government. No one is allowed in the theatre. No props, costumes, set pieces can be removed.

HOUSEMAN

We have an office in the back. I assume we can use that.

SOLDIER

I'll have to check with my commander.

Houseman turns and walks away with his assistant, Augusta.

HOUSEMAN

That's it. Go and check with Stalin, you Cossack stooge.

A car passes, slows down and backs up. The back window rolls down. It is the Countess and Carlo. Augusta and Houseman approach the car.

COUNTESS

Jack. Jack. What is happening?

HOUSEMAN

We've been shut out. The Feds have closed us down.

Aldo Silvano (John Turturro) studies his lines as Larry Foreman before opening night.

John Houseman (Cary Elwes) confronts "the Cossacks" blocking the entrance to the Maxine Elliott Theatre.

COUNTESS
Oh, how exciting.

HOUSEMAN
Listen, darling, I need your help. What are you doing now?

COUNTESS
I'm a busy bunny, Jack. I was headed for an opening at the Metropolitan, and Mr. Mathers, you know he has labor troubles. Tonight there is a masquerade ball at the Vanderheusens. I'm a very busy bunny. What do you need?

HOUSEMAN
I need you to join us in a clandestine operation. Are you game?

COUNTESS
Clandestine. How is it done?

INT. CONGRESSIONAL CHAMBER. DAY.
Hallie sits at a table, a microphone in front of her. Photographers and press members fill a packed room. In the front of the room is a panel of seven congressmen, the Dies Committee on Un-American Activities.

CHAIRMAN DIES
Mrs. Flanagan, you are the first woman in America to receive the Guggenheim Foundation scholarship? Is that correct?

HALLIE
Yes, that is correct.

CHAIRMAN DIES
You went abroad for twelve or fourteen months to study the theatre?

HALLIE
I did.

CHAIRMAN DIES
What date was that?

HALLIE
That was in 1926 and 1927.

CHAIRMAN DIES
You spent most of that time in what country?

HALLIE
In Russia.

CHAIRMAN DIES
In Russia. How much time did you spend in Russia, Mrs. Flanagan?

HALLIE
I spent two months and a half in Russia out of fourteen months. But let me say, gentlemen, that—

CHAIRMAN DIES
Did you spend more time there studying the theatre than you did in any other country?

HALLIE
I did, because there are many more theatres in Russia than there are in any other country.

CHAIRMAN DIES
Did you or did you not make the statement that the theatres in Russia are more vital and important?

HALLIE
Yes, I did find that.

STARNES
What is it about the Russian theatre that makes it more vital and important than the theatres of the continent and the theatres of the United States?

HALLIE
I would be glad to answer that, but before I do I would like to say I have maintained consistently that Federal Theatre is American theatre, American theatre founded on American principles, which has nothing to do with the Russian theatre.

STARNES
I know, but you are not answering the question, Mrs. Flanagan.

CHAIRMAN DIES
Did you make any later trips to Russia to study the theater?

HALLIE
I went to Russia in 1931.

CHAIRMAN DIES
Did you attend the Olympiad there?

HALLIE
I did.

CHAIRMAN DIES
Was this at the time of the Fifth Red Internationale of Labor Unions that you attended?

HALLIE
I wouldn't know that. I was going to see the theatre. That was my one concern.

STARNES
Are you a member of any Russian organization at the present time?

HALLIE
I am not.

STARNES
Have you been a member of any Russian organization?

HALLIE
I have not.

Cherry Jones and Tim Robbins approach the bench to confer during Hallie Flanagan's testimony. Congressman Starnes on the right is played by Gil Robbins, the director's father.

INT. MAXINE ELLIOTT'S THEATRE BASEMENT. DAY.

Sandra hears a knocking on the window. She opens it and lets Houseman and Augusta in. They walk to the office where they encounter Marvel with a spear. Houseman picks up phone.

HOUSEMAN
Hallie Flanagan, please . . . well where in Washington? This is Jack Houseman. My theatre has been seized by Cossacks. I need to talk to her immediately. This is an emergency.

He hangs up.

HOUSEMAN
She's in Washington, testifying.

Welles enters.

WELLES
We're radicals, Jack. Locked out for content. Very exciting.

HOUSEMAN
We need a plan. We've got to think. We need a plan.

WELLES
We'll find a different theatre.

They embrace giddily.

HOUSEMAN
Augusta, get me George Zorn. He's a booker. He'll know the dark theatres.

WELLES
We'll smuggle the costumes out.

HOUSEMAN
The set . . .

WELLES
I hate the set. It's a nightmare. A brilliant idea poorly executed.

HOUSEMAN
I've always said the play would work better on a bare stage.

WELLES
Actually Hallie said that.

HOUSEMAN
I said it first.

WELLES
Fine, Jack, you win, you've got the biggest creative dick.

AUGUSTA
I've got George Zorn on the line.

HOUSEMAN
George, we have a theatrical emergency. Can you come over to Maxine Elliott's Theatre? . . . Now!

INT. WPA OFFICES. DAY.
We start on a radio that broadcasts Hallie's testimony and pull out to see workers listening. Hazel Huffman enters. Her coworkers clearly do not like her. Hazel walks nobly to her post. Someone puts the notice of cuts in front of her, slamming it down.

CLERK
Cuts. Twenty percent. Three thousand people out of work. I sure hope they're all Reds that lose their jobs.

EXT. MAXINE ELLIOTT'S THEATRE. DAY.
The Countess hides behind a gate. Silvano approaches and the Countess pokes her head out and whispers out of the corner of her mouth.

COUNTESS
Don't look at me.

SILVANO
Huh?

COUNTESS
Don't look. Please. Are you an actor?

SILVANO
Yes.

COUNTESS
Cradle Will Rock?

SILVANO
Yes.

COUNTESS
Now listen carefully. Use the back entrance, through the window of the women's dressing room. Good luck. Godspeed.

She disappears. Silvano moves into the alley.

INT. MATHERS'S MANSION (PARLOR). DAY.
Hearst and Gray Mathers.

MATHERS
Roosevelt wants me to give in, follow the rest of Little Steel.

HEARST
He has no spine.

MATHERS
Says if we don't capitulate we'll have a revolution on our hands.

HEARST
A revolution. Ha.

MATHERS
Gradual measures, he says. What do you think, W.H.? You think Lewis has that kind of strength?

HEARST
I think people are poor and angry and will follow anybody that promises them gold. They've got you cornered, Gray. If you give in, you lose money and you open the floodgates to Socialists and radicals. If you resist you will wind up resisting with guns. And that won't look good. Killing strikers doesn't play to the public. You've got to find a way to give them a dollar and take two. Not an easy task.

A pause.

HEARST (*cont'd*)
I still get butterflies when I let go of money like this. Shouldn't. Have plenty. Still gets your heart going.

Mathers gives him one of the parcels wrapped in a brown paper bag.

HEARST (*cont'd*)
Now listen, I am buying art. That is all. If anything comes back to me, I'll bury you and your company.

MATHERS
Not to worry.

Movie still of Maxine Elliott's Theatre, the night Cradle is scheduled to open.

94

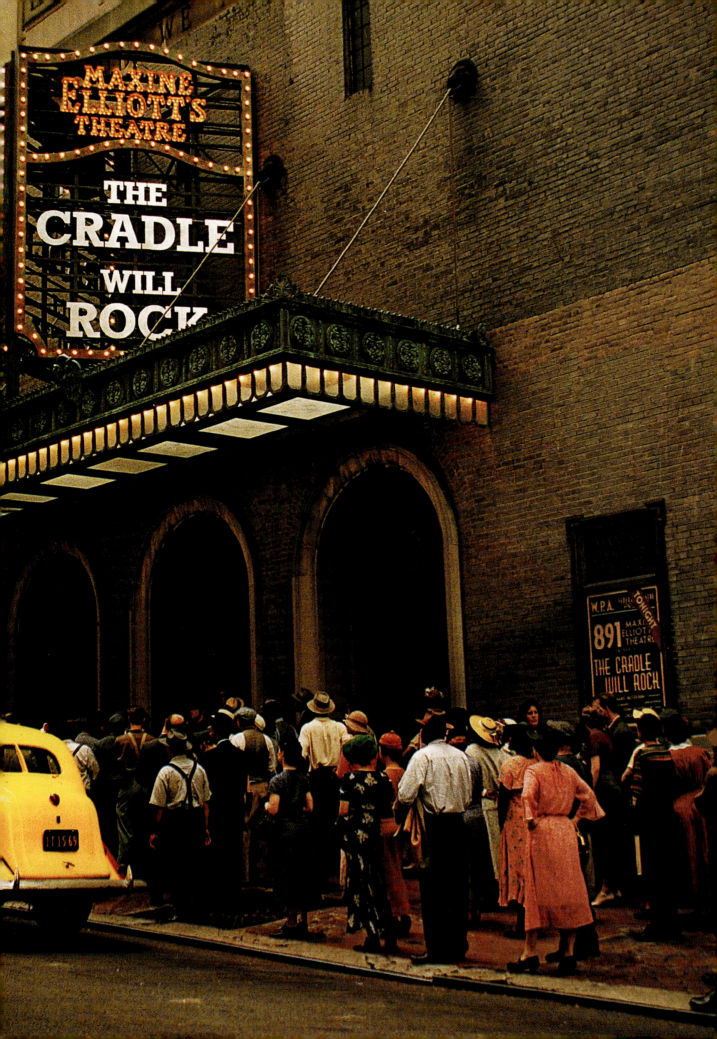

Art & Power: An Uneasy Alliance

William Randolph Hearst and Gray Mathers mix commerce and art.

The use of art as a tool by the politically and economically powerful is a running theme throughout *Cradle Will Rock*. At the same moment as the film depicts Margherita Sarfatti swapping da Vincis for war materials, Mussolini's Nazi counterpart was in the midst of an ideological campaign against modern, and particularly expressionist, art.

In 1937, Hitler emptied Germany's museums of sixteen thousand pieces of "Judeo-Bolshevik" art, many of which he later sold to fund his own military machine. Selected examples from the confiscated works were assembled for a Munich exhibition entitled *Entartete Kunst* ("Degenerate Art") that eventually toured the entire country. The exhibition had a twofold purpose. One aspect celebrated the aesthetic values of Nazism, emphasizing bucolic landscapes and portraits of "pure" Germanic types. These were rendered with unvarying stylistic uniformity in order to convey the impression of having been copied directly from nature—in this case, a nature incapable of producing a leaf out of place or an idiosyncratic face. The purported superiority of such sanitized depictions was used for the exhibition's second purpose: to discredit works that Hitler's minister for visual arts called "the monstrous offspring of insanity, impudence, ineptitude, and sheer degeneracy." The German public was invited to compare and contrast works by expressionist artists such as George Grosz, Paul Klee, and Max Beckmann, with idealized depictions of Hitler Youth on the march, a field full of picturesque peasants, and a pious old man with his head bowed in prayer. In the hands of Nazi artists, the nude became a pretext for advertising "classical" Aryan proportions and reinforcing sexual stereotypes.

Hitler not only admired and collected this sort of art, he had personally painted it in his youth. Though twice rejected from the Vienna Academy of Fine Arts, he had earned a living in his early twenties by rendering Tyrolian mountain scenes and Viennese landmarks and by drawing posters for shopkeepers, including one of a Gothic cathedral spire rising out of a mountain of soap cakes.

The Nazis continued their program of confiscation in the countries they occupied during World War II, and the ownership of many stolen works is still in dispute. By chance, during *Cradle Will Rock*'s filming in New York in 1998, two paintings by Egon Schiele, on exhibition at the Museum of Modern Art (MoMA), were claimed by families whose artwork had been plundered by Nazis, embarrassing the museum and setting off an international incident that has yet to be resolved.

In some of the final scenes of the film, Diego Rivera's mural is shown being smashed to pieces as Hearst and Mathers try to buck up a disconsolate Nelson Rockefeller over drinks upstairs in the Rainbow Room. Hearst exhorts Nelson not to let himself be pushed around by artists who don't know their place. Better to "create the next wave of art. You have the purse strings. It's quite obvious you have the power."

Mathers insists that the next wave be "nonpolitical." Nelson agrees, "Yes, abstract. Colors, form, not politics." And the trio strikes a deal. Rockefeller will fund a traveling exhibition throughout Europe highlighting American artists. Hearst's newspapers will "hail it as the next new thing" and "canonize the artists, make them rich."

Mathers worries that artists will always have political and social concerns. But Hearst assures him that those who won't play the game "won't be seen. And rather than starve, they'll adapt." Then, in a bizarre twist, Hearst echoes Brecht's real-life injunction to Blitzstein: "Artists are whores like the rest of us."

In depicting this fictional moment, Robbins used cinematic sleight of hand to support the historical fact that abstractionism was indeed embraced by members of America's corporate elite during the Depression, and was subsequently used as a weapon in the Cold War. In the ideological contest for European hearts and minds, abstractionism provided an antidote to Soviet-style Socialist realism and demonstrated the colorful and unfettered artistic imagination of the free world. Nor was the eventual triumph of the "avant-garde" over the "realists" hindered by political maneuvers such as MoMA's former executive secretary Thomas W. Braden being appointed head of CIA cultural activities in the early 1950s.

Meanwhile, *Fortune* magazine reported in 1955 that "the art market is boiling with an activity never known before," and listed WPA alumnus Jackson Pollock (who had been fired from the FTP for being a Communist sympathizer) and Willem de Kooning, among others, as "speculative or 'growth' painters." At the same time, a series of promotional exhibitions, most of them sponsored by MoMA, effectively inundated the European art world. In Tim Robbins's *Cradle*, as in real life, William Randolph Hearst and his cronies proved more than capable of seizing the right moment to engineer the truth.

INT. ROCKEFELLER CENTER LOBBY. DAY.

A coterie of security guards stand in the lobby. At the head of the formation, a lawyer. Diego approaches.

LAWYER

Diego Rivera?

RIVERA

Yes?

LAWYER

You must vacate the premises. Your work is complete. Rockefeller Center no longer requires your services.

RIVERA

Fuck off.

Diego runs off, pursued by security guards, and starts to climb up the scaffolding.

INT. MAXINE ELLIOTT'S THEATRE (OFFICE). DAY.

George Zorn works the phone, frantically. Some actors have arrived. People mill about.

GEORGE

No can do on the Jolson Theatre. The owner is in the Berkshires. Can't reach him.

HOUSEMAN

Have you tried the Gossamer Arts?

GEORGE

Closed by the Health Department.

WELLES

Get me the *Tribune*. What's the critic's name there? Never mind. Get me the National desk.

HOUSEMAN

The Rialto?

GEORGE

The owner's a Liberty Leaguer, very conservative. I can try.

HOUSEMAN

Try. I love irony.

WELLES

Yes, this is Orson Welles. Who am I speaking with? . . . Yes, I believe you may be interested to know that for the first time in American history the government has sent armed guards to prevent the performance of a play.

Someone sings and does scales in the background.

INT. ROCKEFELLER CENTER LOBBY. DAY.

Diego Rivera clings to the scaffolding as six guards try to pry him off. Diego calls below.

RIVERA

Frida! Mobilize the Art Students League. Tell them what's happening.

INT. VAUDEVILLE THEATRE BACKSTAGE. DAY.

Crickshaw enters, heading toward his dressing room. He sees the two unfunny Communist comedians, Sid and Larry, standing by the bulletin board. Crickshaw stops, looks at the board. On the board we see a notice that reads "20% cuts in personnel."

SID

News flash. News flash. Twenty percent cuts in personnel. It's curtains for us. All of us. I hear a rumor they're going to close this project down. What do you think, Mr. Turncoat?

LARRY

Mr. Crickshaw, we worked up a little routine; can you look at it? Give us your advice.

CRICKSHAW

You're a Red. I don't talk to Reds.

SID

We're not Red, darling. Pink. Like a flower. We are homosexuals, not Communists. Did you think we were Communists?

LARRY

That's rich.

They both laugh.

Mathers cares little for the Da Vinci obtained by Margherita Sarfatti in exchange for corporate favors in Europe.

SID
C'mon. Watch our act.

CRICKSHAW
Leave me alone.

INT. ROCKEFELLER CENTER LOBBY. DAY.
Diego Rivera is being escorted out of the lobby, followed by the lawyer.

LAWYER
Mr. Rockefeller wanted to convey his feelings of appreciation for your work and despite the fact that the work is unfinished, has instructed me to give you a check for full payment.

He gives Diego the check.

RIVERA
That's it? What happens now? You paint over Lenin's face? Put the face of Hearst on it? Hitler? Then what? You paint over the war, the soldiers. Change them into jolly, drunken English fox hunters? A little bucolic pastoral scene of men on horses chasing after a little fox?

INT. WPA OFFICES. DAY.
The employment office. Long lines. An administrator speaks to the crowd.

ADMINISTRATOR
Listen, folks. Due to cutbacks we will not be hiring at the present time. To save you time and aggravation we suggest you drop off your applications and go home or to the park. We're very sorry.

Angle on Hazel.

Left: Hazel Huffman is given the cold shoulder at the WPA offices where she works. Below: Diego Rivera is led out of Rockefeller Center by security guards.

Final Curtain

Part 4

Long before there was Joseph McCarthy, there was Martin Dies. Outraged by the productions *Power, Revolt of the Beavers*, and most of all, *The Cradle Will Rock*, congressional conservatives launched a frontal attack on the FTP in early 1938. Dies, a Democratic representative from Texas, convened a House Un-American Activities Committee (HUAC) to root out the government officials he saw as "undermining the American system." WPA head Harry Hopkins topped Dies's hit list of purported "Communists and fellow travelers," along with most of Roosevelt's high-ranking New Deal staffers.

New Jersey Republican J. Parnell Thomas—subsequently jailed for defrauding the government—fueled HUAC fever in the pages of the *New York Times*, alleging "startling evidence" that the Federal Theatre was not "only a link in the vast and unparalleled New Deal propaganda machine, but a branch of the Communist Party itself."

Unquestionably, the star of Dies's committee hearings was the disgruntled WPA clerk Hazel Huffman (Joan Cusack). Huffman had been fired from the FTP for reading Hallie Flanagan's mail—under orders, she said, from the WPA's New York administrator. Huffman's testimony offered no concrete evidence of illegality; but her insistence on Flanagan's "Communistic sympathies," coupled with a fervent plea that Dies "clear out the Communists of the Federal Theatre" and put it in the hands of a "good all-round Americans interested in obeying the laws," added up to a show-stopping performance.

Running parallel to the fear of Reds, however, was the FTP's seeming willingness—particularly abhorrent to southern Congressmen—to bring blacks and whites together, both on stage and in the audience. One blond Austrian-born actress testified that she had been asked for a date by a Negro on the project, and that whites and blacks fraternized "like Communists" for social equality and race mixing.

When called before the committee to explain "why only plays with Communist leanings" were produced by the Federal Theatre, Flanagan offered an eloquent defense both of her project's success as a relief effort and its groundbreaking cultural work. But her testimony, lasting only a half day, was purely pro forma. When the Dies Committee sent its report to the full House, six months of hearings had been distilled into a single sentence: "We are convinced that a rather large number of the employees on the Federal Theatre Project are either members of the Communist Party or are sympathetic with the Communist Party."

Just after one A.M. on June 30, 1939, the House Appropriations Committee voted 373 to 21 to terminate funding for the Federal Theatre. Dies and company had skillfully tacked their measure onto a bill reauthorizing broad funding for the WPA, making a presidential veto virtually impossible. Though Roosevelt decried the singling out of "a special group of professional people for a denial of work" as "discrimination of the worst type," he had no choice but to sign. Lasting only four years, the FTP became the only government relief program to be shut down prior to the start of World War II.

Clifton Woodrum, the House Appropriations chair, expressed delight at having finally gotten "government out of the theatre business." But Senator Henry F. Ashurst, a staunch FTP advocate, rebuked his fellow lawmakers: "The stage is art. Art is truth and in the final sum of worldly things, only art endures; the sculptures outlast the dynasty, the colors outlive da Vinci, 'the coin outlasts Tiberius.'"

As Flanagan was clearing out her office, she took a call from a congressman eager to discuss a theatre project for his home state. Flanagan reminded him that there was no Federal Theatre, since "you voted it out of existence." After a stunned silence, the congressman asked, "Was that the Federal Theatre?"

In later years Dies perfected his reputation as one of the nation's most extreme cultural reactionaries. In a foreshadowing of what McCarthy's HUAC would dish out to the "Hollywood Ten" during the cold war, he publicly red-baited entertainment figures, including Joan Crawford, Irving Berlin, James Cagney, and Bette Davis. Though history acknowledges Dies as the architect of the Federal Theatre's downfall, few remember his role in congressional hearings held by the less flamboyant La Follette Committee, charged with investigating corporate strikebreaking and antilabor espionage in the wake of the "little steel" bloodbath. In 1939, with the nation's industry gearing up for war, Dies helped vote down the La Follette Committee's bill outlawing oppressive labor practices. The year 1937 had marked the peak of organized labor's meteoric ascent. Few could have predicted how fast its star would fall.

Dies, As In Death

INT. CONGRESSIONAL CHAMBER. DAY.

CHAIRMAN DIES
Miss Flanagan, how many people do you figure
you had as an audience in the United States for
these plays?

HALLIE
The recorded figure, Congressman Dies, was
something like twenty-five million people.

CHAIRMAN DIES
In other words you have reached approximately
twenty-five percent of our population with your
plays.

HALLIE
Something like that.

STARNES
Mrs. Flanagan, you said in *Theatre Arts Monthly*,
and these are your words I am quoting: "The
workers theatres intend to remake a social structure without the help of money, and this ambition
alone invests their undertaking with a certain
Marlowesque madness." You are quoting from this
Marlowe. Is he a Communist?

HALLIE
I am very sorry. I was quoting from Christopher
Marlowe.

STARNES
Tell us who Marlowe is, so we can get the proper
reference, because that is all we want to do.

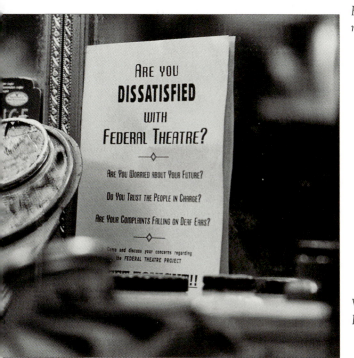

HALLIE
Put in the record that he was the greatest
dramatist in the period of Shakespeare,
immediately preceding Shakespeare.

Laughter. Hallie does not laugh.

STARNES
Of course, we had what some people call
Communists back in the days of the Greek
theatre.

HALLIE
If you say so.

STARNES
And I believe Mr. Euripides was guilty of teaching
class consciousness also, wasn't he?

HALLIE
I believe that was alleged against all the Greek
dramatists.

STARNES
So we cannot say when it began.

HALLIE
Wasn't it alleged also of Ibsen and against
practically every great dramatist?

STARNES
I think so. All right. That is all I have to ask,
Mr. Chairman.

EXT. MAXINE ELLIOTT'S THEATRE. DAY.

*A crowd has gathered. Welles, Houseman, and
Blitzstein approach the Countess on their way to
meet the press.*

WELLES
Countess, we need a piano.

COUNTESS
A piano?

WELLES
In case the theatre we find doesn't have one.

COUNTESS
Good thinking.

WELLES
Find us a piano. Here's ten dollars. That should
cover the rental. Marc, we need a piano. Tell the
Countess where she might find one.

*Welles and Houseman continue toward the press as
Blitzstein stays with the Countess.*

WELLES
We most assuredly will be performing *The Cradle Will Rock* tonight.

REPORTER
Where? What theatre?

HOUSEMAN
We are currently negotiating with three theatres. We will let you know within the hour.

EXT. ROCKEFELLER CENTER. DAY.
A group of young people has gathered. Diego Rivera is there. People mill about.

YOUNG MAN
Why can't we go in?

GUARD
This is private property. It is not open to the public.

YOUNG WOMAN
We want to see the painting.

GUARD
The lobby is closed.

YOUNG WOMAN
Let us in.

VOICES
Down with Rockefeller.

INT. ROCKEFELLER OFFICE. DAY.
Rockefeller paces in his office. A Robespierre costume waits on a hanger nearby. Three men in custodial clothing stand near the door.

MENDEZ
No es fresco. Es muy formidable.

SOL
The paint will come through.

MENDEZ
Must hit.

SOL
Chip.

ROCKEFELLER
Chip?

Rockefeller's secretary, Claire, enters.

CLAIRE
Nelson, the masquerade party starts in a half hour. You wanted me to remind you.

ROCKEFELLER
Not now, Claire. Sol, do we have a pneumatic drill?

INT. MAXINE ELLIOTT'S THEATRE. DAY.
Marvel sits with Silvano running lines.

MARVEL
You're Larry Foreman.

SILVANO
Ex-foreman.

MARVEL
I've been looking all over town for you.

SILVANO
Well, how's the union returns, Mr. Mister?

MARVEL
Oh, damn it. What is it?

We move off them to find a chaotic scene as actors, musicians, and technicians mill about.

DULCE
Has anyone asked the WPA if this is OK?

We see Welles, Houseman, Blitzstein and Augusta.

AUGUSTA
Jack, we've got trouble with the actors' union. They won't sanction a performance elsewhere.

HOUSEMAN
What?

AUGUSTA
The actors' union is forbidding the actors from performing.

INT. MATHERS'S MANSION (PARLOR). DAY.
Gray Mathers is talking on the phone while being dressed in his eighteenth-century costume.

MATHERS (*on the phone*)
You're damned right. Mathers Steel will not be intimidated. Just a second . . .

James, the driver, has entered. Mathers covers the mouthpiece of the phone.

MATHERS
Where the hell is my wife?

JAMES
I last saw her at Maxine Elliott's Theatre on 39th Street, sir.

MATHERS
You left her there?

The deadly serious political theatre of the Dies committee unleashed one spontaneous burst of hilarity. In a case of mistaken identity as madcap as a scene from Shakespeare's *Midsummer Night's Dream*, the bard's fellow Elizabethan playwright Christopher Marlowe was transformed into a Communist.

The son of a shoemaker, Marlowe was born in Canterbury in 1564. By the time an innkeeper killed him in a sword fight over his bar tab at age 29, Marlowe had flourished as a poet and translator. His first play, *Tamburlaine*, earned him a reputation as a master of the "mighty line." His other dramas included *Dr. Faustus*, *The Jew of Malta*, and *Edward II*, and it is possible that Marlowe and Shakespeare collaborated on *Titus Andronicus*, *Henry IV*, and *Richard III*.

Along the way, Marlowe revolutionized the stage conventions of his day. His plays mark a shifting away from highly stylized verse toward gripping, character-driven drama organized around a single, psychologically complex personality. Marlowe wrote for the passionate and violent times he lived in. But his powerfully rendered protagonists had the ability to time-travel and emerge in the midst of a Welles-Houseman production dramatically intact. The anguish of Marlowe's doomed antihero erases the centuries to evoke a universal present:

> *Where art thou, Faustus? Wretch, what hast thou done?*
> *Damned thou art, Faustus, damned; despair and die!*
> *Hell claims his right, and with a roaring voice*
> *Says, "Faustus, come; thine hour is almost come";*
> *And Faustus now will come to do thee right.*

But Marlowe was not above writing farce into his tragedies, as in the scene where Faustus lends his enchanted horse to a simpleton with instructions not to ride it over water under any circumstances. Knowing (along with Faustus) that a fool will do exactly what he is told not to, the audience anticipates the moment when the chastened horseman returns half drowned and blubbering. On touching water, however, the horse is transformed into a bale of hay.

By attempting a blanket indictment of the FTP, the Dies Committee was itself grasping at straws, riding roughshod over Marlowe's far-from-Communistic focus on the consequences of moral choices made by individuals. How then might the playwright have reacted to the following real-life dialogue between the Dies Committee's Representative Joseph Starnes and Hallie Flanagan over her assertion in print that the Federal Theatre possessed "a certain Marlowesque madness"?

Christopher Marlowe, author of the original Faustus.

Mr. Starnes: This Marlowe, is he a Communist?

Mrs. Flanagan: I am very sorry. I was quoting from Christopher Marlowe.

Mr. Starnes: Tell us who Marlowe is, so we can get the proper reference, because that is all that we want to do.

Mrs. Flanagan: Put in the record that he was the greatest dramatist in the period immediately preceding Shakespeare.

Mr. Starnes: Of course we had what some people call Communists back in the days of the [ancient] Greek theatre, and I believe Mr. Euripides was guilty of teaching class consciousness also, wasn't he?

Mrs. Flanagan: I believe that was alleged against all of the Greek dramatists.

Mr. Starnes: So we cannot say when it began. . . .

Though Starnes inadvertently made a laughingstock of himself and HUAC, he did succeed in raising into high relief the unease felt by his fellow conservatives about the passion for social change that drama can, and often does, arouse. Flanagan herself had written that "drama, through rhythmic speech, dynamic movement, and contagious listening, can influence human thought and lead to human action." A threatening concept, indeed.

Christopher Marlowe: Communist

JAMES

She dismissed me, sir.

MATHERS

Bring the car around.

James leaves.

MATHERS (*back to phone*)

Are we clear? That's right, whatever it takes.

The butler enters.

BUTLER

Miss Sarfatti to see you, sir.

MATHERS

Show her in.

Carlo is lounging as usual.

MATHERS

Carlo, privacy please. Why don't you go clean the toilets or something?

CARLO

I clean nothing.

Sarfatti enters. Greetings in many languages until:

MATHERS

Out, everybody out!

SARFATTI

Oh, Gray, did you receive the package?

MATHERS

Yes, yes I did.

SARFATTI

You did not open it?

MATHERS

No, I haven't.

SARFATTI

Well?

Mathers begins to open the parcel.

SARFATTI

And Mr. Hearst, did he receive his package?

MATHERS

Yes, he did.

*Her job done, Sarfatti leaves Rockefeller Center. "I think she
has real misgivings," Sarandon says of her character. "In her
heart of hearts she knows that these great pieces of art are going
to end up in the homes of people who don't appreciate them,
who don't love them. And it upsets her."*

SARFATTI

Did it please him?

MATHERS

Yes, very much.

SARFATTI

Ah.

MATHERS

When do you sail?

SARFATTI

Tonight.

MATHERS

Your payment, madam.

SARFATTI

Thank you. And Mussolini thanks you.

MATHERS

We, I, we are going to miss you.

SARFATTI

You did not tell me what you feel.

MATHERS

About you?

SARFATTI

About the painting. You open it but you say nothing.

MATHERS

Oh. I love it. It's a masterpiece. It's a Da Vinci.

SARFATTI

Where will you hang her?

MATHERS

In the study. Above the fireplace.

SARFATTI (*quietly*)

What a shame to let the classics slip away.

INT. MAXINE ELLIOTT'S THEATRE (BASEMENT). DAY.
Adair picks up the phone.

WELLES

They won't reconsider?

BLITZSTEIN

They won't even talk about it. The bastards,
Fascists.

HOUSEMAN

Well, that's it, isn't it?

WESTON

What is it? What's going on?

WELLES

The final nail.

AUGUSTA

Actors' Equity says no.

HOUSEMAN

The fire curtain falls.

HIRAM

No to what?

WELLES

Why do you always try to best me?

BLITZSTEIN

We can't do the show.

HOUSEMAN

What?

WESTON

What?

WELLES

Best my metaphors. Final nail. Fire curtain. I hate you, Jack.

AUGUSTA

We can't do the show. Equity says.

HOUSEMAN

I hate you, too.

GEER (*to Sandra*)

Have you ever loved me?

WELLES

I catch you saying things I've said. Word for word. Plagiarism.

SILVANO

No musicians? How will we do the show without musicians?

HOUSEMAN

Of course. I owe my entire education to you.

ADAIR

The show is off.

BLITZSTEIN

This play is doomed. It's me. I'm unlucky. This is my fault.

DULCE

What?

Making desperate calls to find an alternate theatre where they can perform Cradle.

WELLES

But we're not dead yet.

SILVANO

I know that. I could tell by the padlocks on the front door.

HOUSEMAN

We are indeed dead. There will be no show tonight.

ADAIR

Not the government, the union.

WELLES

I say black you say white. I say stop you say go. You're an evil man.

SILVANO

The union?

MARVEL

What's the reason?

CANADA LEE

The steel unions?

GEORGE

Excuse me.

ADAIR

No, our unions say we can't do the show.

OLIVE

Why? What reason do they give?

DULCE

No!

HOUSEMAN

It's a rule.

ADAIR

A rule's a rule.

MARVEL

A rule?

FEDER

They're Nazis. This is censorship.

GEORGE

Excuse me.

ADAIR

Shut up, Abe.

HOUSEMAN

Not now, George. Since you have been paid by the Federal Government in rehearsal you cannot perform the play for another management.

OLIVE

So what does this mean?

MARVEL

That's ridiculous.

ADAIR

It means it's over. It's over, everybody. No show. Time to go home. Let's go, Olive, this play is a disaster.

HOUSEMAN

We thought so, too.

FEDER

What if we do it anyway?

GEORGE

Excuse me.

SILVANO

And get kicked out of the union? Not be able to work? My little $26 a week keeps my family fed. I can't risk it.

DULCE

This is so sad.

GEORGE

Excuse me.

WELLES AND HOUSEMAN

What?!!

GEORGE

I found a theatre. The Venice 59th and 7th. The owner wants a hundred bucks.

HOUSEMAN

Tell him no.

GEORGE

What?

HOUSEMAN

It's over.

COUNTESS

Jack, Jack, I found a piano. Where am I going?

HOUSEMAN

We're not doing the show. We've been censored.

COUNTESS

Well, I have a piano and there's a crowd out there. What if we did it on the street?

HOUSEMAN

We have a theatre. The actors have been forbidden.

COUNTESS
Well, what if Marc did it?

WELLES
By himself?

BLITZSTEIN
What?

WELLES
All the characters?

HOUSEMAN
He did it for us.

WELLES
I know, but it's not going to be any good.

BLITZSTEIN
What's not going to be any good?

WELLES
And besides, he's in the union.

HOUSEMAN
Marc, are you in the musicians' union?

BLITZSTEIN
No. Why?

INT. CONGRESSIONAL CHAMBER. DAY.

CHAIRMAN DIES
You have established the precedent of exhibiting a play championing the cause of ownership of public utilities. You said that was proper and you yourself thought you had a right to do that?

HALLIE
I think so.

CHAIRMAN DIES
Then on the other hand if the same play proved that the public ownership of railroads was a good thing you would do it, too, would you not?

HALLIE
Absolutely, and the test is, is it a good play and within the general range and the variety we have established.

CHAIRMAN DIES
And if someone came with a play showing that public ownership of all the property in the United States, and it was a good play, you would also exhibit that, would you not?

HALLIE
Well, that is a very clever move on your part, to maneuver me into a certain position.

CHAIRMAN DIES
I do not pretend to any cleverness.

HALLIE
No, I would not. We would stop at that, because that would be recommending the overthrow of the United States Government, and I do not want that, gentlemen, whatever some of the previous witnesses have intimated.

CHAIRMAN DIES
In other words you would favor doing it by degrees, but not all at once, isn't that right?

INT. WPA OFFICES. DAY
Hazel is leaving for the day. People turn their backs to her.

HUFFMAN
I want you all to know that I resent the silent treatment, the subtle torture you are all subjecting me to. It is not easy being the one that stands up and says the truth. You all know that there are Communists amongst you, you all know that you date Negroes, you all know that you are anti-Fascist. I say the pox on you and your house. I will not tolerate this abuse.

She turns and exits.

Left: Hallie Flanagan proves too articulate a witness for the committee's comfort. Below: Robbins and his crew capture the tension from behind the congressmen's bench.

INT. VAUDEVILLE DRESSING ROOM. DAY.
Crickshaw applies makeup at the mirror, as the dummy sits motionless next to him.

DUMMY
What a hero you are. Mister "Noble, rat on his friends, now everybody gets fired" Crickshaw. What a hypocrite. You believed in something once, Tommy.

CRICKSHAW
Shut up.

DUMMY
Where have you come, Tommy Crickshaw? Where's the young comrade I once knew? Let's do the old act. One more time? For old times' sake? Come on, Tommy.

EXT. MAXINE ELLIOTT'S THEATRE. DAY.
Silvano flags down his family, who have come to the show.

SOPHIE
What is happening?

SILVANO
They've shut down the show.

SOPHIE
Who?

SILVANO
The union. The government.

Above: Houseman, Blitzstein, and Welles lead the crowd up Broadway toward the Venice Theatre. Right: The Silvano family joins them.

HOUSEMAN
Marc Blitzstein, the composer of *The Cradle Will Rock*, not being a member of the union, will perform the play by himself on the stage of the Venice Theatre twenty-one blocks north on 59th and 7th. You all of course are invited to join us.

DULCE
Where is it?

HIRAM
59th and 7th. Are you going?

WESTON
I don't think so.

DULCE
We should go for Marc.

HOUSEMAN
Every major newspaper critic in New York is here, Marc. Don't let them down.

WELLES
You'd better be good, Marc. Archibald MacLeish, Arthur Arent, Elmer Rice. A thousand people. This is big.

Marvel gets in a taxi.

MARVEL
The Rome Theatre, 57th and 9th.

The taxi leaves.

OLIVE
We should support Marc. He'll be terrified playing alone.

ADAIR
The union has forbidden us from performing this show. If we go to this theatre we could lose our jobs. Now I'm leaving. Either come now or find a different place to sleep.

OLIVE
You're kicking me out?

ADAIR
Come now or sleep somewhere else. Understand?

They leave.

INT. CONGRESSIONAL CHAMBER. DAY

CHAIRMAN DIES
Mrs. Flanagan, we have had a long day and your testimony has been most illuminating. We will adjourn for the evening. We will hear from Mr. Alsberg in the morning.

A gavel hits. The hearing is over.

HALLIE
Just a minute, gentlemen. Do I understand this concludes my testimony?

CHAIRMAN DIES
We will see about it tomorrow.

HALLIE
I would like to make a final statement, if I may, Congressman Dies.

CHAIRMAN DIES
Mrs. Flanagan. It is very late. We'll see about it tomorrow.

HALLIE
Chairman Dies, this Committee has heard testimony for five months now from unqualified witnesses. As head of the Federal Theatre I must insist on more time to refute this testimony. It is only fair and decent, sir.

CHAIRMAN DIES
Let's not talk about decency, Mrs. Flanagan. Federal Theatre is hardly the judge of that. Excuse me, ma'am.

He rushes past. A reporter catches up with Hallie.

Despite her protests, Flanagan is dismissed after only six hours of testimony.

REPORTER
Mrs. Flanagan, any comment on the proceedings?

HALLIE
They are chasing ghosts. I hope to further repudiate these charges tomorrow.

HALLIE
What's going on here, Harry?

HOPKINS
You made Starnes look like a fool and he's furious. Marlowe, a communist. You won the day.

HALLIE
You have to talk to Roosevelt. They have to allow me to continue.

HOPKINS
Oh, you're not getting asked back here.

HALLIE
I had six hours. Hazel Huffman had three days.

HOPKINS
You're embarassing them.

HALLIE
She's a clerk. I'm head of the project.

HOPKINS
You brought intelligence and reason to these

proceedings and this committee is not interested in reason and intelligence.

HALLIE
I must be allowed to continue. You have to talk to Roosevelt.

HOPKINS
This is a show. This is their show and they're writing you out of it.

HALLIE
Did you hear me?

HOPKINS
Did you hear me?

HALLIE
Roosevelt can make it happen. One press release and I'll be back here in the morning.

HOPKINS
This is not going to happen.

HALLIE
What are you saying?

HOPKINS
This is not going to happen. Roosevelt is saving his fights. This is politics, Hallie. Give a little, get a little.

INT. ROCKEFELLER OFFICE. DAY.
A futurist painting we recognize from the art exhibit hangs above the desk of Nelson Rockefeller, who, in costume,

stands admiring his recent acquisition. Margherita Sarfatti is with him.

ROCKEFELLER
Exquisite.

SARFATTI
Congratulations, Nelson. It's you. A beautiful fit.

ROCKEFELLER
You know the next time I see you, we'll probably be at war.

SARFATTI
I hope not. I hope that is avoidable.

ROCKEFELLER
Probably not. Probably not.

INT. ROCKEFELLER CENTER LOBBY. DAY.

The lobby now empty except for the three custodial workers we saw in Rockefeller's office. They are climbing the scaffolding. Sarfatti exits bags in hand.

EXT. ROCKEFELLER PLAZA. DAY.

A protest has formed. The Art Students League hold a sign, "Art Killer." Sarfatti exits, fights her way through the crowd. Diego steps in front of her.

DIEGO
Your friend Rockefeller shut me out.

SARFATTI
Lenin in a capitalist lobby? Oh, Diego, what were you expecting?

DIEGO
I was dragged out of the building like a common criminal.

SARFATTI
You were hired to do a job and now your boss does not like what you did. If you want to create art and comment on revolution, do it at your own expense. Go paint a mural for nothing at the Young Communists League.

DIEGO
Because I take Rockefeller's money now I am his slave?

SARFATTI
Yes.

DIEGO
When did you stop supporting artists?

SARFATTI
I support your art but that does not mean I must support your revolution.

DIEGO
It's the same thing.

SARFATTI
No, it is not.

DIEGO
What a lie you live, a Jewish Fascist.

SARFATTI
And you, a wealthy Communist.

DIEGO
Maintenant, la bataille commence!

As Sarfatti exits, mounted police approach the protesters.

EXT. BROADWAY. DAY.

What seem like a thousand people are marching up Broadway headed to the Venice Theatre. There is no militancy in this march. It is more like a group of people headed to a picnic. People laugh, dance, sing. A parade. Silvano and family, musicians, Welles, and Houseman argue. Blitzstein worries.

CHANCE
Why were the soldiers there?

SILVANO
They were scared that we would steal costumes.

JOEY
They're your costumes.

SILVANO
No, actually the government owns the costumes.

Rivera and Sarfatti accuse each other of hypocrisy.

115

Countess La Grange (Vanessa Redgrave) is swept up in the moment.

Welles himself flew to Washington in an attempt to free up the logjam but to no avail. Federal guards blockaded the Maxine Elliott Theatre, seizing the props and scenery. "The Cossacks," as Houseman called them, even confiscated actor Howard da Silva's toupee as government property.

With ten thousand advance tickets already sold, Welles and Houseman pushed ahead on the seemingly insane assumption that somehow the show would go on. Just as time was running out, they learned that the Venice Theatre on 59th Street was available and led an audience of twelve hundred on a twenty-block parade north. There, Blitzstein—sitting alone on stage at an upright piano, before a fading backdrop of the Bay of Naples left over from the previous show—was preparing to sing his entire musical solo. A Fascist flag hung over the audience of the Italian theatre. As the now-excited crowd waited for the performance to begin, one athletic young man climbed up and ripped it down, to the deafening cheers of the others in attendance.

Most of the cast members were relief workers whose jobs, already on the line, would have certainly been lost if they defied WPA orders. And their union, Actors' Equity, forbade its members from appearing onstage in the disputed show. Blitzstein—not a member of any union—was only a few bars into Moll's first song when Olive Stanton's voice began to rise, at first shakily and then with increasing vigor, from the audience. Abe Feder's spotlight picked her out of the crowd, and soon other actors followed suit, popping out of their seats on cue. Eventually most of the cast joined da Silva's balding Larry Foreman in belting the final chorus as the audience roared its approval:

> When you can't climb down,
> And you can't say "No!"
> You can't stop the weather,
> Not with all your dough!
> For when the wind blows . . .
> Oh, when the wind blows . . .
> The cradle will rock!

In cinematically re-creating *Cradle*'s wildcat premiere, Tim Robbins scheduled the shooting of this climactic scene for the final round of principal photography. Just before rolling the cameras, he took the stage to give the actors, and more than a thousand extras, a brief background on the show that galvanized the American stage.

But Robbins purposely left off just short of Olive Stanton's heroic intervention, hoping to capture on film the spontaneity of the 1937 opening-night triumph. With the cameras rolling, the "audience" of extras responded with unrehearsed delight, applauding at some of the least expected moments, laughing at even the most subtle lines. Several of the principal actors—including Hank Azaria as Marc Blitzstein, who said it was a moment he'd "never forget"—turned in what they consider to be the performance of their lives.

Part of what made the FTP

a target for conservative attacks on the New Deal as a whole was its irrepressible, rebellious spirit. Nowhere was this more evident than when Blitzstein's *The Cradle Will Rock* surged beyond the control even of WPA administrators.

In June 1937, just as *Cradle* was set to open, Congress was considering the possibility of 25 to 30 percent cuts in the WPA's white-collar division. To forestall any controversy that might prejudice the debate, WPA top brass summarily canceled *Cradle*'s premiere: no Federal Theatre productions were to open before July 1.

> **66** There had always been the question of how to produce a labor show so that the audience can be brought to feel that it is part of the performance. This technique seems to solve the problem and is exactly the right one for this particular piece. **99**
>
> —*Marc Blitzstein, after the initial spontaneous performance of* The Cradle Will Rock

The Grand Finale

CHANCE
Why did they have guns?

SILVANO
Seems strange, doesn't it?

JOEY
So you're not doing the show?

SILVANO
The government says we can't.

JOEY
But you want to do it?

SILVANO
Yes.

JOEY
Is it against the law?

SILVANO
No. But they're my boss. And they pay me, and they say we can't do the show.

JOEY
But you still want to do it so why don't you do it?

SILVANO
Because I can't. It's been forbidden. And I could lose my job.

EXT. VENICE THEATRE. DAY.
Gray Mathers arrives, in his eighteenth-century costume, as a piano is being hoisted by firemen into the stage door of the new theatre.

MATHERS
Constance, what on earth are you doing?

COUNTESS
I'm getting the piano off the truck. Oh my heavens, darling, I was supposed to meet you at home an hour ago. I have failed you miserably. I do hope you will forgive me. You look splendid. Gray, darling, have you any money? I'd like to give these generous men a gratuity.

MATHERS
Get in the car.

COUNTESS
Why, my dear?

MATHERS
We are going.

COUNTESS
But darling, we'll miss the play.

MATHERS
Certainly my intention.

COUNTESS
Oh no, dear, this is too exciting an evening. Please don't ask me to choose between Marie Antoinette and this evening. I'd never forgive you if I missed the performance tonight.

And we see, coming down the block, a thousand people.

MATHERS
Good Lord, it's a revolution. Get in the car.

COUNTESS
It's the audience!

The Countess laughs and pulls Gray into the car.

INT. ROLLS ROYCE. DAY.

COUNTESS
Carlo, please give my husband and me some privacy.

CARLO
Nyet, merci.

Carlo stays.

COUNTESS
When did you ever get to be such a stick-in-the-mud?

Gray opens the door.

MATHERS
Stop it. We're going home. My wife has gone completely mad.

Countess opens the other door and gets out of the car.

MATHERS
Get in, now!

COUNTESS
Perhaps you have mistaken me for a spaniel.

MATHERS
Get in or I'll cut off your allowance.

COUNTESS
You'll do nothing of the kind. And if you do I'll have to live as a gypsy lives.

She turns on her heels and heads toward the theatre. Gray shuts the door and the car leaves.

INT. VAUDEVILLE THEATRE STAGE. DAY.
Crickshaw is on stage, performing an impromptu act.

CRICKSHAW

Times must be hard when I look at you and see firewood.

DUMMY

Kindling I couldn't even . . . hey, what are you saying?

CRICKSHAW

Why, my oaken friend, Mr. Roosevelt has laid us off.

DUMMY

Cutbacks?

CRICKSHAW

Politics.

DUMMY

I told you, you shouldn't have ratted on my friends.

CRICKSHAW

Friends?

DUMMY

Ooops.

CRICKSHAW

Did you say friends? Those Reds are your . . .

DUMMY

Sorry, Comrade.

CRICKSHAW

Comrade?

DUMMY

We are all brothers and we will not rest until all the country is Red.

CRICKSHAW

I've known this dummy like the back of my hand. In my own hand a revolutionary!

DUMMY

Ladies and gentlemen, this man exploits my labor for his own profits. This capitalist pays me zero, works me whenever he likes. I sleep in a coffinlike apartment.

At times during its production, the movie *Cradle Will Rock* intersected uncannily with the history on which it is based. One notable instance was the way Robbins ended up shooting his climactic final scenes in Broadway's Brooks Atkinson Theatre. Originally a theatre in suburban Tarrytown, New York, had been chosen, but only six extras showed up for the casting call. The search then shifted to New York City, where extras abound but where securing an empty theatre is tougher than finding a taxi at rush hour.

The night the funeral procession for Tommy Crickshaw's dummy Melvin was being shot in Times Square, Robbins and production designer Richard Hoover ducked into the Brooks Atkinson to use the facilities and discovered that a show had unexpectedly just closed there. Within a few days, the historic playhouse was transformed into a credible look-alike for the Venice Theatre, circa 1937. What lent this happenstance special significance was that the Brooks Atkinson was named for one of theatre's preeminent critics who, despite his abhorrence for *Revolt of the Beavers*, had gone on record as one of the FTP's staunchest supporters.

Born in 1898, Justin Brooks Atkinson was hardly a critic with his head in the clouds. Though firmly anti-Communist, he nonetheless lent his name and energies to fundraising efforts on behalf of the anti-Fascist cause during the Spanish Civil War. And he warned Hallie Flanagan early on that the FTP was certain to produce politically volatile theater. Given the tenor of the times, it was "naïve to assume that any form of public expression would be innocuous. Particularly in

Our Mr. Brooks

the case of unemployed citizens; they could not be neutral about a world which had rejected them."

Atkinson's erudition and appreciation of the American theatre's range and diversity became a hallmark of the *New York Times* during a tenure that began in 1925 and lasted, with a brief interruption during the war years, until 1960. His praise for Blitzstein's *Cradle* as a show which "raises a theatregoer's metabolism and blows him out of the theatre on the thunder of the grand finale," conferred much-needed legitimacy on its success.

Though the Dies Committee used his anti-*Beavers* review as evidence of the FTP's Communistic leanings, Atkinson's defense of the project in the *Times* left no doubt as to his sentiments: "Federal Theatre seems like boondoggling to a congressman who is looking for a club with which to belabor the administration and there is always something that can be blown up into a scandal. But for socially useful achievement, it would be hard to beat the Federal Theatre, which has brought art and ideas within the range of millions of people all over the country. It has been the best friend the theatre as an institution has ever had in this country."

When Atkinson died in 1984, he himself was counted among the irreplaceable pillars of the institution he loved so well.

Brooks Atkinson, critic for the Times *for almost four decades, and a film shot (left) of the re-created Venice Theatre.*

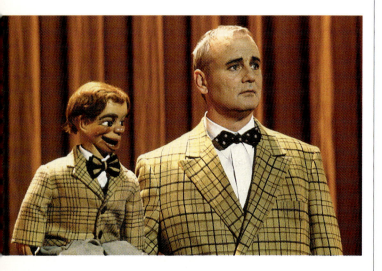

The last straw for Tommy Crickshaw: even his own dummy turns out to be a Red.

CRICKSHAW
You're a dummy.

DUMMY
Dummies. This is what he calls us, Brothers and Sisters. If it is dummies we are then I say dummies rise up. Rise up to the proletarian call of dummies everywhere. Storm the barricades. Riot in the streets.

The dummy begins to sing "L'Internationale." Hazel watches from the audience. Crickshaw finishes and exits, leaving the dummy alone on stage.

INT. CONGRESSIONAL CHAMBER. DAY.
Rose and Hallie pace. De Rohan and O'Hara sit in chairs. The chamber is empty.

ROSE
Are we through? Is this it?

O'HARA
Should I be looking for a job?

HALLIE
We've got another year if we fight.

ROSE
You know I can understand the puritans. I can understand the politics but I guess I don't understand the passion of it. The intensity of the anger.

HALLIE
It's not just anger. It's fear.

O'HARA
Fear?

Hallie sits at the dais.

HALLIE
Mr. O'Hara, have you ever heard of Michael Grunwald?

O'HARA
Was he a Communist?

HALLIE
No. Mr. De Rohan?

DE ROHAN
Michael Grunwald. An historian. Elizabethan England. Not a Communist as far as I know.

HALLIE
Mr. O'Hara, have you read any of his books?

O'HARA
No, Congressman Flanagan. I skipped that course.

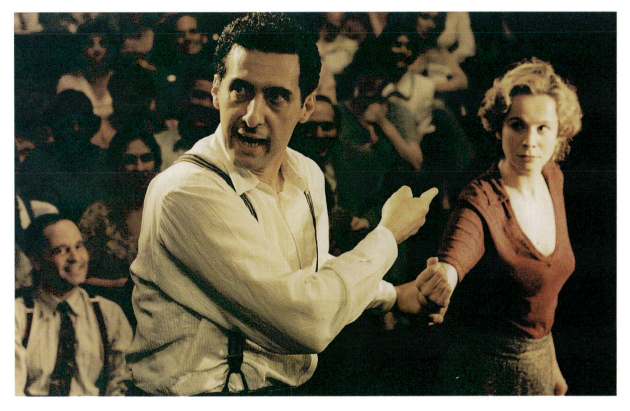

Aldo Silvano and Olive Stanton lead the renegade performance of The Cradle Will Rock.

HALLIE
But you know your history of Elizabethan England?

O'HARA
Well, yes, from Shakespeare.

HALLIE
From a playwright. I see. Mr. O'Hara, who was Richard III?

O'HARA
A humpback and a killer.

HALLIE
Mr. De Rohan, what is Michael Grunwald's opinion of Richard III?

DE ROHAN
Much maligned; a great ruler.

HALLIE
And yet this Shakespeare has written a play that is still performed while Mr. Grunwald's books gather dust. Would you consider that unfair, Mr. De Rohan?

DE ROHAN
Why, yes. I would say that this Mr. Shakespeare should be investigated.

HALLIE
And if all else fails we can remove his words. Burn them.

Pause.

ROSE
We're not painting pretty pictures. It must scare the hell out of them.

O'HARA
Well, the plays are written. They're here forever.

HALLIE
I hope they are.

A pause.

HALLIE
Federal Theatre's going to end but theatre's going to be better off. We've launched a ship. A grand and glorious ship.

INT. VENICE THEATRE. DAY.
As the audience assembles at the new theatre an Italian flag that had been hanging in the theatre is torn down by Abe Feder. The crowd cheers. Silvano sits with his family.

JOEY
Why'd they do that?

SILVANO
Ask your uncle. That's his flag.

Vicky Clark, playing Dulce Fox, rises from the audience.

The Countess is sitting next to Canada Lee, talking with him. There is a palpable buzz in the theatre, a nervous energy. Olive Stanton appears and we follow her. Dulce sees her and calls.

DULCE
Olive! Here.

Olive sits.

OLIVE
Hi.

DULCE
I thought you went home.

OLIVE
I don't have a home now.

DULCE
He kicked you out?

OLIVE
Can I sleep on your floor tonight?

DULCE
Sure.

OLIVE
I didn't want to miss this.

INT. RAINBOW ROOM. NIGHT.
The masquerade ball of the rich and famous to benefit the

Museum of Art *is in full swing. We see Rockefeller, Hearst, and Mathers.*

HEARST
What in God's name were you expecting from a Communist?

ROCKEFELLER
He wasn't my first choice. I wanted Picasso or Matisse.

HEARST
We control the future of art because we will pay for the future of art. Appoint people to your museum boards that detest the Riveras of the world. Celebrate the Matisses. Create the next wave of art. You have the purse strings. It's quite obvious you have the power.

ROCKEFELLER
Cultural power.

HEARST
Yes.

ROCKEFELLER
Pay for the Matisse.

HEARST
Celebrate color.

MATHERS
Celebrate form.

HEARST
Portraits.

MATHERS
Countrysides.

ROCKEFELLER
Men on horses.

MATHERS
Sunsets.

ROCKEFELLER
Nudes.

INT. VENICE THEATRE. NIGHT.
The audience is all abuzz.

WELLES
Ladies and gentlemen, welcome to the first runaway production of the Federal Theatre. I'm sure you are aware by now of the circumstances that have led us here to this dusty theatre on this beautiful summer night. Something in this play frightens people in Washington. There must be

some sinister force at work in this play, so without further ado I would like to introduce you to the monster behind *The Cradle Will Rock*: Mr. Marc Blitzstein.

Blitzstein enters and sits at the piano.

BLITZSTEIN
Good evening. Fade to black. We are in Steeltown, USA. A prostitute walks down the street. This is Moll. She sings.

(sings)
I'M CHECKIN' HOME NOW,
CALL IT A NIGHT.
GOIN' UP TO MY ROOM,
TURN ON THE LIGHT.
JESUS, TURN OFF THAT LIGHT.

We hear a woman's voice, at first weak, restrained. It is Olive standing from her chair in the audience.

MOLL (OLIVE)
I AIN'T IN STEELTOWN LONG.
I WORK TWO DAYS A WEEK;
THE OTHER FIVE
MY EFFORTS AIN'T REQUIRED.

We see Welles, astonished.

MOLL (OLIVE)
FOR TWO DAYS OUT OF SEVEN
TWO DOLLAR BILLS I'M GIVEN;
SO I'M JUST SEARCHIN' ALONG THE STREET. . .

Will Geer cranes his neck to see Olive.

MOLL (OLIVE) *(cont'd)*
FOR ON THOSE FIVE DAYS IT'S NICE TO EAT.
JESUS, JESUS, WHO SAID LET'S EAT?

In the back of the house we see Adair, fuming.

BLITZSTEIN
Enter a well-dressed gentleman.

Pause. No response. Adair leaves the theatre. No Gent.

BLITZSTEIN
Enter a well-dressed gentleman on the make.

Still no response.

BLITZSTEIN
Enter me.

GENT (BLITZSTEIN)
I'd like to give you a hundred bucks, but I only got thirty cents.

INT. RAINBOW ROOM. NIGHT.

HEARST
Nelson will fund the new wave of art. A traveling exhibit throughout Europe highlighting American artists.

Tim Jerome, Chris McKinney, Erin Hill, and Daniel Jenkins join in the act.

"Say Goodnight, Gracie"

The Lights Go Down on Vaudeville

By the mid-1930s, vaudeville acts like this one were being eclipsed by movies and radio.

Just down the block from the Mansfield (the playhouse that in 1960 would be renamed for Brooks Atkinson) stood the Palace Theatre. Built in 1913 on the corner of 47th and Broadway, the Palace served—until its conversion to the silver screen in 1932—as the heart of vaudeville. Here, for a modest admission, audiences could take in slapstick comics, jugglers, and trained animal acts—all accompanied by musicians from nearby Tin Pan Alley, where music publishers and shops selling instruments still cluster today.

At a typical Palace show, the crowd might grow misty-eyed as a tenor warbled "Maggie Cline, the Irish Queen." But it was left to Sophie Tucker, the queen of

vaudeville, to reduce even the stone-hearted to helpless tears, pulling out the stops on "My Yiddisha Mama." For laughs, there were young Borscht Belt–honed comics like Jack Benny (born Benjamin Kubelsky), Danny Kaye (born David Daniel Kominski), and George Burns (born Nathan Birnbaum), who later teamed up with Gracie Allen to form their famous comedy duo.

From its beginnings following the Civil War and lasting through the advent of sound film in the late 1920s, vaudeville developed its own distinct form of American popular culture. With the theatre divided along class lines—the upper crust attending the opera and classical musical concerts—vaudeville's broad, unpretentious fare was claimed by the white urban masses.

Drawing on traditions as diverse as African-American dance, British music-hall entertainment, and Yiddish theatre, vaudeville provided a ready commercial outlet for ethnic cultural forms. For the most part, performers of color played only the most stereotypical onstage roles. But there were rare exceptions, such as jazz great Eubie Blake, for whom vaudeville provided a springboard to even greater subsequent success. It also served as a proving ground for talents such as Moss Hart, Clifford Odets, John Garfield, Tony Curtis, Bob Hope, Shelley Winters, the Marx Brothers, and Jan Peerce, as well as many others who would later achieve prominence in "legitimate" theatres and concert halls, or the movies.

And the pay wasn't so shabby either, at least for the top bananas. In vaudeville's heyday, circa 1920, a star performer like Fanny Brice could earn as much as $2,500 a week playing New York's "subway" circuit, or touring the national network of some nine hundred vaudeville theatres. But by the mid-thirties, with the increasing popularity of radio and the movies, vaudeville had fallen into sharp decline. Many theatres had converted to cinemas or closed altogether. Although the Federal Theatre sought to revive the form by establishing special variety show units and underwriting apprenticeships, its audience had all but vanished.

In Robbins's movie, the fictional Tommy Crickshaw represents this venerable tradition reeling on its last legs. Crickshaw's character bears some resemblance to the real-life Frank Merlin, an irascible Roosevelt-hating entertainer whom Hallie Flanagan picked to head the FTP vaudeville unit. "Is it a hard job and does it pay anything?" was all Merlin wanted to know before accepting the position and, in effect, putting his art form on the dole.

The demise of the FTP also brought down the curtain on vaudeville's nearly fifty-year run. But its spirit survived—initially on the radio variety shows that drew in so many of its alumni, then later on television, with Milton Berle, Jack Benny, and Sid Caesar, and still later on *The Ed Sullivan Show* and *Laugh-In*. Into the late 1970s, traces of vaudeville could be found in the madcap sketches and novelty acts of *The Tonight Show Starring Johnny Carson*.

MATHERS
Nonpolitical.

ROCKEFELLER
Yes, abstract. Colors, form, not politics.

HEARST
My papers will hail it as the next new thing. We will canonize the artists, make them rich. Before long all artists will be doing the next new thing.

MATHERS
Do you think? There's something about artists that always gets socially concerned.

HEARST
Sure. But they won't be paid for it. They'll have no influence. They won't be seen. And rather than starve, they'll adapt.

MATHERS
It's survival.

HEARST
And artists are whores like the rest of us.

They all laugh.

INT. VENICE THEATRE. NIGHT.
We see Aldo Silvano seated next to his kids. As Welles takes Olive, she sings:

MOLL (OLIVE)
MAYBE YOU WONDER WHAT IT IS,
MAKES PEOPLE GOOD OR BAD;
WHY SOME GUY, AN ACE WITHOUT A DOUBT,
TURNS OUT TO BE A BASTARD,
AND THE OTHER WAY ABOUT.
I'LL TELL YOU WHAT I FEEL:
IT'S JUST THE NICKEL UNDER THE HEEL . . .

INT. ROCKEFELLER CENTER LOBBY. NIGHT.
The scaffolding is back up. The three workers have a pneumatic drill turned upside down. They are chopping into the wall, tearing into the Diego Rivera artwork.

MOLL (OLIVE) (V.O.)
GO STAND ON SOMEONE'S NECK
WHILE YOU'RE TAKIN';
CUT INTO SOMEBODY'S THROAT AS YOU PUT—
FOR EVERY DREAM AND SCHEME'S
DEPENDING ON WHETHER,
ALL THROUGH THE STORM . . .

INT. VENICE THEATRE. NIGHT.
Olive now in the balcony, concludes the song.

MOLL (OLIVE)
YOU'VE KEPT IT WARM . . .
THE NICKEL UNDER YOUR FOOT.

Spontaneous applause erupts. The audience is electrified.

BLITZSTEIN
Scene two. A holding cell. Moll sits there depressed as Larry Foreman, a union leader is thrown in there with her. He says . . .

Pause. An awkward long silence. We see Silvano.

Blitzstein, seeing no one rise, begins to perform. Then a groan. Slowly Silvano rises from his seat.

LARRY (SILVANO)
O-o-o-h, boy! I just been grilled. Say, who made up that word, grilled?

She sees his face.

MOLL (OLIVE)
Ooh, you been hit good.

LARRY (SILVANO)
You're new here. What's the matter? They catch you on the streets?

MOLL (OLIVE)
Uh huh. Whatta they got you for?

LARRY (SILVANO)
Who, me? Makin' a speech and passin' out leaflets! The fawmal chahge is Incitin' to Riot— Ain't you ever seen my act?

We see Joey, eyes wide open, a defining moment in this child's life. We see Sophie and Chance.

LARRY (SILVANO)
Well, I'm creepin' along in the dark; my eyes is crafty, my pockets is bulging! I'm loaded, armed to the teeth with leaflets. And am I quick on the draw! I come up to you . . . very slow . . . very snaky; and with one fell gesture—I tuck a leaflet in your hand! One, two, three—there's a riot. You're the riot. I incited you. . . . I'm terrific, I am!

BLITZSTEIN
Scene three, Night Court. Enter the Liberty Committee.

No one moves.

SILVANO
Saaay, what's the whole Liberty Committee doin' in a night court? And on the wrong side of the bar?

No one moves. Silence. A buzz from the audience.

EDITOR DAILY (BERT)
Think of what my people would think if they could see me!

MRS. MISTER (DULCE)
You know Mr. Mister. He'll come and bail us out.

EDITOR DAILY (BERT)
Phone to Mr. Mister. To come and bail us out.

MRS. MISTER (DULCE)
We're the most respectable families in the city!

SANDRA AND GEER
We're Steeltown's Liberty Committee!

Hiram stands up, terrified.

EDITOR DAILY (BERT)
We're against the union! We're against the drive!

DR. SPECIALIST (HIRAM)
Why, I drew up the manifesto: "Steeltown is clean, Steeltown is a real town."

HIRAM, BERT, DULCE, SANDRA, CANADA, GEER
"We don't want a union in Steeltown!"

Now Canada Lee stands up; it's become a steamroller. There's no turning back.

REV. SALVATION (CANADA)
I am the Reverend Salvation. We have formed the Liberty Committee to combat against Socialism, Communism, Radicalism, and especially Unionism.

EDITOR DAILY (BERT)
I'm the editor of the *Steeltown News*.

DR. SPECIALIST (HIRAM)
I'm his personal doctor!

MRS. MISTER (DULCE)
I'm Mr. Mister's personal wife. Mr. Mister's Mrs. Mister.

SISTER MISTER (SANDRA)
I'm his daughter, Sister Mister.

JUNIOR MISTER (GEER)
And I'm his son, Junior Mister.

MOLL (OLIVE)
Who is this Mr. Mister?

LARRY (SILVANO)
Better ask who he's not. He owns steel and everything else.

LIBERTY COMMITTEE
So, Mr. Mister, please take pity. Come and save your pet committee from disaster.

They come from their seats and move towards the front of the stage. Six musicians have also joined in, playing their parts from their seats.

JUDGE (HOUSEMAN)
Order. Order. First case. Name.

LARRY (SILVANO)
Reverend Salvation.

MOLL (OLIVE)
Habitual prostitute since 1915.

We hear the Salvation Song as we cut to:

INT. ROCKEFELLER CENTER LOBBY. NIGHT.
A girl being beaten by a cop on horseback starts disintegrating, being chipped away by Rockefeller's workers.

EXT. VAUDEVILLE THEATRE. NIGHT.
The two unfunny comedians, Sid and Larry, have made a small coffin for the dummy, which lays, elevated, in front of the theatre. Lit candles surround the coffin; the two men stand next to it in solemn attention like an honor guard at a state funeral. A crowd has gathered.

INT. VENICE THEATRE. NIGHT.
Song ends. Applause erupts. The audience is electrified, looking everywhere. Actors are all around. Anything can happen.

After its triumphant

premiere, *The Cradle Will Rock* ran for another eighteen performances at the Venice before moving on to the Windsor Theatre for 108 more, sans props, and with Blitzstein still solo at the piano. Now officially off the government payroll, Welles and Houseman broke up Project 891 and started the Mercury Theatre before parting company for good. Once ensconced in Hollywood, Welles wrote a screen treatment, never produced, of Blitzstein's landmark musical.

Olive Stanton, who had come out of nowhere to appear on history's stage, stood up to dramatic acclaim, then disappeared with equal mystery. After *Cradle* closed, she maintained her Actors' Equity status, paying dues until 1940, when she simply dropped off the radar. Will Geer parlayed his portrayal of the villainous Mr. Mister into a series of sinister movie roles. Late in his career,

Left: Howard da Silva as Larry Foreman and Olive Stanton as Moll in the night court scene of the Mercury Theatre production of The Cradle Will Rock, *late 1937. Above: Cary Elwes and Hank Azaria take their curtain calls as John Houseman and Marc Blitzstein.*

Geer reversed his typecasting with a long-running TV role as Grandpa Walton, the wise and benevolent patriarch of a Great Plains family struggling through the Depression.

Howard da Silva, born Howard Silverblatt, went on to star in dozens of movies and Broadway shows after he riveted audiences in the role of Larry Foreman. Called to testify before HUAC's postwar reincarnation under Joseph McCarthy, da Silva invoked the Fifth Amendment, refused to name names, and was blacklisted and shut out of his profession for years.

When the Federal Theatre itself folded, Hearst's *Herald Tribune* sounded a smugly triumphant note. Other papers, including some that had whipped up a headline frenzy during the Dies Committee hearings, decried the "slaughter" and declared the FTP's closing "a catastrophe" and "a tragedy." One of the few genuinely sincere epitaphs to appear was offered by the independent *Brooklyn Eagle*, which had covered virtually every production and mourned the loss of "a finer, more vital national theatre than any country in the world has ever had before, a theatre as cheap as the movies and yet with the marrow of ideas in it."

"A Grand and Glorious Ship"

Near the end of the movie *Cradle Will Rock*, Hallie Flanagan parts company with her staff and their shared goal of creating an enduring national theatre by declaring: "Federal Theatre is going to end, but theatre's going to be better off. We've launched a ship, a grand and glorious ship."

Indeed, a raft of FTP alumni, including actors Burt Lancaster, Joseph Cotten, and E. G. Marshall; directors Joseph Losey, Sidney Lumet, and Elia Kazan (who later cooperated with HUAC, naming several former colleagues as Communist sympathizers); and composer Virgil Thomson, subsequently established notable, long-term careers in Hollywood. Jules Dassin, who performed in *Revolt of the Beavers*, went on to act and direct movies for MGM. In the late 1940s, with the advent of the McCarthy witch-hunt, Dassin exported his considerable acting and directorial talents to Europe and appeared with Melina Mercouri in the sixties' classics *Never on Sunday* and *Topkapi*.

One of Dassin's fellow beavers was Perry Bruskin. With the founding of the FTP, Hallie Flanagan invited Bruskin's already-established company, Shock Troupe, to become its first experimental theatre unit. Alternating between roles in children's and adult productions, Bruskin was acting in George Sklar's *Life and Death of an American* when funding was abruptly cut.

Bruskin continued on in theatre as an independent actor and producer, and directed Brendan Behan's *The Hostage,* which opened on Broadway in 1960. Currently he is producing a film documentary on the experimental and labor stage in the "dark ages" before the Federal Theatre. Bruskin, now in his eighties, generates a vitality enviable in a man of thirty. And he retains his passion for the WPA years—"the golden era of culture in America" —historically unparalleled for "the murals, the art, the music, the plays . . . for the courage it gave to the black theatre community."

"Did you ever hear of a little town named Brobdignag, Arkansas?" he asks. "Well I haven't either. It doesn't exist. But if it did, the WPA would have been there, with theatre—real, professional theatre—for people who had never seen anything like it before."

But what Bruskin recalls most vividly was his work with "the kids." During *Beavers*'s first performances, Bruskin remembers, there was a resounding silence after the last scene ended—just rows and rows of awestruck eyes. "It was the first theatre many of them had ever experienced. They didn't realize they were supposed to clap."

And as for the woman who oversaw it all? After four years as the nation's most public impresario, Hallie Flanagan returned to the relative tranquillity of academia. In 1940 she published *Arena*, a forthright and frequently humorous memoir of the tumultuous times that rocked the American stage. The ferment the FTP stirred up with its bold, unconventional productions continues to spur the imaginations of veterans like Bruskin, as well as dramatists, actors, and directors of all ages as they seek to extend the boundaries of their art.

Hallie Flanagan died in 1969, just about the time that Liang Tee Tue was born. In 1989 Ms. Tue, a graduate student in the Film and Theatre Department of Hunter College of the City University of New York, turned her master's thesis on the Federal Theatre Project into a fully scripted Living Newspaper. In one scene—a madcap satire of the Dies Commission—when a congressman asks Hazel Huffman to define "social significance," she snaps back, "Communist propaganda!" Later, as the mock HUAC hearings draw to a close, Mickey Mouse himself stands accused of being a Red, based on a misinterpretation of the origins of the word "mouse."

One can almost hear Hallie Flanagan laughing with delight as she must have some sixty years ago during the *Cradle* moment, watching the beavers rise up in revolt.

Above: Hallie Flanagan (Cherry Jones) looks to the future. Right: The young Burt Lancaster, here with co-performer Nick Cravat, began his long acting career as an aerialist with the circus division of the FTP.

EDITOR DAILY (BERT)
Mr. Mister, you got here at last!

SISTER MISTER (SANDRA)
Oh, you don't know what we've been through!

DR. SPECIALIST (BERT)
These idiots don't know us!

Hiram, now playing Mr. Mister, approaches, script in hand.

MR. MISTER (HIRAM)
You're Larry Foreman.

We hear a voice.

VOICE
You're Larry Foreman.

The actors turn. It is Marvel. Terror on his face. Will he remember his lines?

LARRY (SILVANO)
Ex-foreman.

MR. MISTER (MARVEL)
I've been looking all over town for you.

LARRY (SILVANO)
Well, how's the union returns?

MR. MISTER (MARVEL)
(*Tentatively, slowly remembering.*) They haven't come to a decision yet. Mr. Foreman, I know a lot about you, you were once in my employ. Look here . . . we're both for the same thing, a fair and square deal for everybody. Why don't you persuade your union to join with the Liberty Committee into one big united organization.

He looks above.

MARVEL (*cont'd*)
Thank you.

LARRY (SILVANO)
Let me understand you. . . . You'd like my services in swinging your way all the people I've signed up, all the people who agree with the union. You want me to change their mind, is that it?

MR. MISTER (MARVEL)
Well that's a little strongly put.

LARRY (SILVANO)
Ought to be worth quite a sum to you, eh?

MR. MISTER (MARVEL)
I thought so. You needn't worry about that part. I'll see you get what it's worth. Let's talk it over outside.

LARRY (SILVANO)
Wait! I'm kinda funny that way. I'd like to know now about how much it might be worth?

Mr. Mister writes a figure on a slip of paper and hands it to Larry. In the audience we see Joey, Silvano's son.

LARRY (SILVANO) (*cont'd*)
You don't say. Worth that much to you, hmm? Well, you take all that money and go buy yourself a big piece of toast.

The audience cheers. We see Joey, eyes full of pride, the future.

LARRY (SILVANO)
Now, then, get out of here. And take this little girl with you! Out there she doesn't cost you nothin'; in jail you're liable to have to feed her!

MR. MISTER (MARVEL)
Why, you goddamned skunk! I'll break you . . . I'll run you out of town . . .

LIBERTY COMMITTEE (ALL)
Kill him! Lynch him!

LARRY (SILVANO)
Yeah, lynch, kill! Listen once and for all, you scared bunch of ninnies! Outside in the square they're startin' somethin' that's gonna tear the catgut outta your stinkin' rackets! That's Steel marchin' out in front! But one day there's gonna be wheat and sidewalks, cows and music shops, houses, poems, bridges, drugstores. The people of this town are findin' out what it's all about. They're growin' up! And when everybody gets together like Steel's gettin' together tonight, where are you then? Listen, you Black Legions, you Ku Kluxers. You Vigil-Aunties hidin' up there in the cradle of the Liberty Committee. When the storm breaks; the cradle will fall! (*a horn sounds*) Listen! The boilermakers are with us! (*a clarinet*) That's the boilermakers' kids! They done it.

Beat of drums and the sound of voices singing "Upon the Topmost Bough."

COP (BLITZSTEIN)
They're marchin' down here! They got no permit to march!

JUDGE (HOUSEMAN)
Arrest them!

129

COP (BLITZSTEIN)
Arrest them? There's thousands of 'em! They're standin' in front of the courthouse, right here!

MR. MISTER (MARVEL)
My God! What do they want with me?

INT. VAUDEVILLE THEATRE DRESSING ROOM. DAY.
Crickshaw sits stone-faced looking at himself in the mirror. A strange frozen joy on his face, a deep sadness in his eyes. A knock on the door. He opens it. Hazel Huffman is there. They embrace.

EXT. CITY STREET. NIGHT.
The two comedians are now leading a procession of about forty people through the streets of New York. On their shoulders they carry the coffin. A short man in front of them carries a sign which says: "Federal Theatre. Born 1934, Died 1937. Killed by an act of Congress."

INT. ROCKEFELLER CENTER LOBBY. NIGHT.
The mural continues to be demolished.

INT. VENICE THEATRE. NIGHT.

ALL SING (V.O.)
UPON THE TOPMOST BOUGH
OF YONDER TREE NOW,
LIKE BEES IN THEIR HIVES,
THE LORDS AND THEIR LACKEYS AND WIVES
A SWINGIN' "ROCKABYE BABY" IN A NICE BIG
    CRADLE.
THEN THEY REMARK THE AIR
IS CHILLY UP THERE.

INT. ROCKEFELLER CENTER LOBBY. NIGHT.
A face comes plummeting down and shatters on the marble floor.

INT. VENICE THEATRE. NIGHT.

ALL (V.O.) *(cont'd)*
THE SKY BEETLE-BROWED;
CAN THAT BE A CLOUD OVER THERE?
AND THEN THEY PUT OUT THEIR HANDS AND
    FEEL STORMY WEATHER!

INT. ROCKEFELLER CENTER. NIGHT.
Another chunk of art plummets.

INT. VENICE THEATRE. NIGHT.

ALL (V.O.) *(cont'd)*
A BIRDIE UPS AND CRIES . . .
"BOYS, THIS LOOKS BAD;
YOU HAVEN'T USED YOUR EYES;
YOU'LL WISH YOU HAD."

INT. ROCKEFELLER CENTER. NIGHT.
We see one of the workers as he chips the art, tears in his eyes.

INT. VENICE THEATRE. NIGHT.

LARRY (SILVANO) AND CAST
(singing)
THAT'S THUNDER,
THAT'S LIGHTNING,
AND IT'S GOING TO SURROUND YOU!
NO WONDER THOSE STORMBIRDS
SEEM TO CIRCLE AROUND YOU!

INT. ROCKEFELLER CENTER. NIGHT.
The workers continue to drill into the Diego Rivera artwork.

LARRY (SILVANO) (V.O.)
WELL, YOU CAN'T CLIMB DOWN,
AND YOU CAN'T SIT STILL.

EXT. CITY STREET. NIGHT.
The funeral procession for Crickshaw's dummy continues.

INT. VENICE THEATRE. NIGHT.

LARRY (SILVANO) (V.O.)
THAT'S A STORM
THAT'S GOING TO LAST UNTIL
THE FINAL WIND BLOWS . . .
AND WHEN THE WIND BLOWS . . .
THE CRADLE WILL ROCK!

All of the cast from various parts of the audience stand and sing:

ALL
THAT'S THUNDER,

We see Canada Lee singing.

ALL
THAT'S LIGHTNING,
AND IT'S GOING TO SURROUND YOU!

We are close on Olive Stanton.

ALL
NO WONDER THOSE STORMBIRDS
SEEM TO CIRCLE AROUND YOU!

We see the Countess enraptured.

ALL
WELL, YOU CAN'T CLIMB DOWN,
AND YOU CAN'T SAY "NO"!

Welles and Houseman sing along.

ALL
YOU CAN'T STOP THE WEATHER,
NOT WITH ALL YOUR DOUGH!

FOR WHEN THE WIND BLOWS . . .
OH, WHEN THE WIND BLOWS . . .

We see Olive Stanton triumphant.

ALL
THE CRADLE WILL ROCK!

The spot illuminating Silvano blacks out. The audience sits in silence for a second and then . . . erupts. Ecstatic applause. Cheers, war whoops, a tumult of appreciation.

We see Marc Blitzstein jumping up and down, hugging Welles.

The accordion player who has been accompanying Blitzstein starts to play an upbeat number.

Welles starts to stamp on the stage with his foot, a wild

dance. Olive Stanton joins him. The audience begins to pound their feet and clap their hands.

The pounding has reached a fever pitch. People dancing and cheering.

We see the Countess doing a jig. We see Olive Stanton, her arms upraised, yelling in jubilation.

EXT. STREET. NIGHT.
We see the funeral procession of the dummy, then pull up on crane to see modern-day movie set, klieg lights, extras, traffic held, Times Square.

THE END

The funeral procession for the dummy—and the Federal Theatre—that closes the film.

Notes on the Making of the Film

by Tim Robbins

At the beginning of *Cradle Will Rock* a title appears: "A (mostly) true story." This is a film, and in the interest of storytelling I bent some facts and manipulated some dates. The Rivera-Rockefeller controversy actually occurred in 1932, the invasion of Ethiopia in 1935, the downfall of the Federal Theatre in 1939. I invented the characters of Mathers, Countess La Grange, Carlo, Aldo Silvano, and Tommy Crickshaw and his nemeses, Sid and Larry. The rest of the characters in this film are based on real people and are as historically accurate as possible.

The portrayals of Orson Welles and John Houseman are based on accounts of people who knew them at the time, and I have tried to bring their precocious genius to life without overromanticizing them. Whether Margherita Sarfatti actually sold classical art to the elite in the United States cannot be known for certain, but we do know that she was a stalwart defender of Fascism and an active propagandist for Mussolini. We may never know the complete truth about where confiscated art wound up after World War II, but we do know from recent lawsuits that many of these pieces are now in private collections.

Likewise, I have tried to portray Nelson Rockefeller and William Randolph Hearst accurately, although some of their actions in the movie represent metaphorical leaps. There is no way to know exactly what goes on in the back rooms of power—one can only take the deplorable facts (Hearst's support of Mussolini and Hitler, Rockefeller's destruction of the Rivera mural) and fill in the rest with one's imagination.

THE SHOOT

Our first feet of film were of the glorious newborn face of the Silvano baby. There were to be many very tough days ahead during the shoot, but I have selective amnesia when it comes to the negative. There were such incredible moments of joy, of ecstasy, of creative wonder; so many glorious images flash through my mind as I remember those three months. The experience of filming *Cradle Will Rock* reignited my love for theatre, for actors, for writing, and filled me with inspiration day after day. So many surprises lay in store for us.

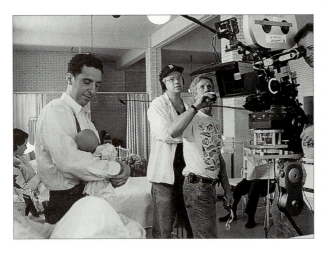

First shot: the Silvano family with their new arrival.

The great onscreen chemistry of Angus Macfadyen and Cary Elwes; the slow, sexy tango of Ruben Blades with his Frida, Corina Katt (a woman we hired as an extra who proved to be a fine actress); the willing and joyous dancing of Diego's models and the wild abandon of a slightly looped young Rockefeller (John Cusack). There was the mixed emotion and regret on Sarfatti's (Susan Sarandon's) face as with cash in hand she looks at Diego's mural; the baby who cried on cue in the Silvano bed; the Beavers; the plate spinner; the puppets. And there was the day we worked twenty-two hours to destroy the mural, slept one hour, then began shooting again. What a crew we had! The collective creativity and stamina on that set was mind-boggling. If I could live my life shooting this film again and again, it would be too rich, too exciting, too tiring a life.

THE CREW

I was blessed with a remarkable team of artists and craftspeople on *Cradle Will Rock*. I had been talking with Richard Hoover, our production designer, for years about the project, and when it became a reality, Richard dove in with an all-consuming energy. This was more than a job for him; it was a way for him to bring his love of the theatre to the screen. He was not only bringing thirties New York to life but also the groundbreaking direction and lighting design of the young Orson Welles; the elegance and beauty of artworks, from modernist canvases to the sprawling Rivera mural; and the moneyed back rooms and mansions of the corporate elite. Richard was courageous enough to give us street scenes of strangeness and iconoclasm, and at the same time design the fantasy in the brilliant but addled mind of Marc Blitzstein with equal relish and detail.

Ruth Myers (left), with some of her designs for the dummy funeral procession.

Likewise, in her costume design, Ruth Myers was able to show the incredible range of economic worlds of the time, bringing style and panache to the moneyed classes, yet never shying away from the holes and patches in the costumes of characters who hadn't been able to buy new clothes in twenty years. Too often, I believe, period films look too damn nice. The clothing tends to be well pressed, beautifully coordinated, freshly dry-cleaned. Ruth took darning needle in hand and distressed the look, creating a subtle, worn aesthetic for the film. She also showed wit and Felliniesque flair in the costumes of the singing Beavers, the vaudevillians, and the mourners in the funeral procession at the end of the movie. Both Ruth and Richard created their magic within the constraints of an impossible budget, showing incredible ingenuity in overcoming their lack of funds.

The cinematographer, Jean Yves Escoffier, created an elegant, gritty look that captured both the poverty and the integrity of those times, so essential to the spirit of the movie. He was also efficient and fast in his lighting, which was invaluable given our daunting schedule. I hired Jean Yves for his past work and incredible talent, but most important, for his honesty. When I interviewed him for the job, I told him I hadn't liked the content of one of the movies he had done. He defended the film proudly, not backing down from the art he had created in an effort to get the job. I want people around me who believe passionately in their work, who bring to the table their beliefs and idiosyncrasies and who aren't afraid to express them. Ultimately, it is up to the director to choose from among the different opinions, to create a unified

Jean Yves Escoffier, cinematographer.

vision. In my case, that vision would have been impossible to attain without people like Jean Yves, Richard, and Ruth—and this film had the good fortune of their talents.

Another invaluable member of the creative team was David Robbins. Before David would write one note of the score, he had to find a way for the various musical components of the film to gel. The film incorporates music from start to finish, from the opening fanfare of the newsreel behind Olive Stanton to the music she hears in the alley; from the first strains of Blitzstein's piano to the orgiastic finale. David was constantly trying to figure out such details as: What songs would be playing on Diego Rivera's radio? How does the music from *Cradle* evolve from composition, to rehearsal, to the orchestration used at the opening per-

Composer David Robbins, left, rehearses with actors
from Revolt of the Beavers.

formance? In actual fact, only the accordion player joined Blitzstein that night at the Venice Theatre. But Blitzstein had written brilliant orchestrations, and David realized that to hinge the end of the movie simply on the piano and accordion would not do justice to the music. We took the liberty of creating a renegade band of musicians who show up at the theatre and play. David's decision on which instruments to include elevated the music, I believe, and consequently the climax of the movie. Once filming was completed, David drew on Gypsy music, Eastern European songs, and American jazz to create a lively and celebratory score.

Tod Maitland, our sound mixer, managed up to twenty-four body mikes at a time and gave us well-balanced, clear tracks. Our cameraman, Jim McConkey, showed the strength and resilience of a bear, whether perfecting the intricate moves on a track or maneuvering his steadycam in the tight confines of backstage dressing rooms. His crowning moment came early on the third day of filming, in the opening shot of the movie. Jim started with his camera inside the theatre, went down a steep staircase, backward and uphill into an alley, onto the street, up onto a crane, through a window, and into Blitzstein's apartment, ending on a close-up of the composer's sheet music on the piano! Again and again, Jim was able to deliver the impossible when we needed it.

In editing the film, Geraldine Peroni contributed her outstanding sense of rhythm and discerning eye. While crafting the movie's pace, Gerry remained open to experimentation and was not afraid to make bold choices. She helped me through a torturous and obsessive process, and did so with an ease and grace that was a delight to be around.

THE CAST

"What a cast!" is generally the reaction I get when I tell people about this movie. Doug Aibel, the casting director, and I worked for an inordinately long time casting the movie. Not only were there a great number of roles, there was also the challenge of casting historical figures. Many wonderful actors who were considered for parts seemed too modern for this context; they didn't suit the tone we were striving for in the film. Bob Balaban, Susan Sarandon, Vanessa Redgrave, and John Turturro were chosen long before we started the casting process. They all had been instrumental in early readings of the script, and I developed their parts for them. Joan Cusack, whom I've known for years and whom I'd just worked with in Houston, came aboard as Hazel Huffman. And her brother John, one of my co-conspirators in the Actor's Gang (an experimental theatre group we started in the early eighties), despite a hectic schedule of back-to-back films, generously managed to squeeze us in between.

Bill Murray came on board pretty late in the process. I was lost with this role for a while, originally thinking the character Tommy Crickshaw would be much older. It was Doug who suggested Bill, and coincidentally he appeared on *David Letterman* that week. Letterman asked Bill if he thought he'd ever win an Oscar—Bill said he figured he'd win the Heisman Trophy before he'd win an Oscar. He was very funny as always, and as I watched the show Crickshaw began to present himself as a younger man. I'm a great believer in coincidences and happenstance. Shortly afterward, I sent Bill the script with a note saying, "Here's your Heisman."

Most of the other actors in *Cradle* auditioned at some point. I wish I was more self-assured and could cast a movie without auditioning; it's my least favorite part of the process. Why? Because in my heart I'm an actor. I know how hard it is to walk into an office and try to impress a director enough for him or her to cast you. You try your best, you open up emotionally to complete strangers sitting behind a desk who, more often than not, have a hundred reasons *not* to cast you: You're too tall, not famous enough, not pretty enough, not the right type, ad infinitum. Having been in the position of judge myself, I can tell you that the decision of who plays what role has little to do with the talent one shows in an audition. There is an intangible something that separates the one you cast from the others—it's a feeling, an instinct, and yet it is solid and intractable. The actor walks out of the room and you say, "That's the one." I couldn't begin to tell you why.

As an actor reading this explanation, I feel no solace, only resentment.

When you consider that close to a hundred people are seen for any given role, you as a director are doling out much more disappointment than happiness. I hate casting; it makes me miserable and depressed.

THE GRAND FINALE

Near the end of the schedule, we had one huge hurdle to overcome. In the last week of filming we had to capture the renegade performance of *The Cradle Will Rock*. This is where the whole project had started. It didn't matter what we had done up until this point; if we didn't pull this off, we didn't have a movie. How would the audience of extras respond to this play? Could it have the same relevance to them that the original had? How many shots of the actors would be ruined by a bored or indifferent audience member? This audience had to be on fire—we had to create electricity in that theatre or we were dead. On top of this pressure, we had decided early on that we would film eight musical numbers and several scenes from the play in addition to what was in the film script—in other words, we had to shoot the equivalent of sixty pages in one day.

The actors were primed, ready. We had rehearsed and choreographed everything. I had hired Broadway pros that could handle the pressure. Three cameras sat on tracks onstage and two were hidden in the audience. One thousand extras sat in period clothing in the Brooks Atkinson Theatre.

Being an extra is hard work. It must be horrible to sit around in wool clothes on a summer day and have some person with a walkie-talkie barking orders at you. Unfortunately, as a director you don't have much control over that sort of thing, but on this day—with the demands we had and the need for magic to happen—I talked to these people as if they were the most important actors on the set that day. I gave everyone a brief history of the time period. I told them that they had gone to the Maxine Elliott Theatre twenty blocks downtown, that there were locks on the door, guards outside with guns. There was something dangerous happening. The play had something to do with a steel strike. Two weeks ago police killed ten people and injured sixty in a Chicago labor riot. It was front-page news, and the cries of outrage had been building since. Spontaneous strikes have

Robbins sets the stage for the audience of extras.

been erupting throughout the city.

So you march uptown, I told them. You find yourself in this theatre. There are police around. Given the climate of the times, what you are doing could be considered a subversive act. There is a good chance that people could get hurt in here. I did not tell them that actors would be standing up among them and performing the play from the audience.

What would ensue in that day of shooting was unlike anything I had ever experienced. We had time for only one pass on each piece. Cameras were aimed toward the audience, I was perched at the monitors with Jean Yves, trying to guide these five cameras to capture spontaneous moments. The room came alive when Emily Watson stood up. There was a look of absolute terror, but also quiet determination, on Emily's face. Bolts of

Olive Stanton (Emily Watson) rises to sing.

energy seemed to fly through the theatre. It was there, electricity. By the time Turturro stood up, the place was on fire. It was remarkable. John seized the moment, played off the excitement in the room, and gave a performance as labor leader Larry Foreman that still sends chills through me. The audience responded with total spontaneity. They got the jokes, even ones I didn't think were there. They delighted in the spectacular performances of Henry Stram, Tim Jerome, Dan Jenkins, and Erin Hill. They responded most strongly to the Salvation Song, following its quite complicated structure and brilliant antiwar sentiments, laughing at topical references from 1914. Inspired by stellar performances from Chris McKinney and Vicky Clark, the theatre erupted in applause. I could not have wished or prayed for a better result. By the time Barnard Hughes entered as Mr. Mister, the place was sky high, and as he and the others performed the finale, I swear the place near levitated. Not once on that day did I instruct anyone to laugh here or clap there. What you see on film is a real event, as close as I could ever have hoped to come to that evening in June 1937.

PROSTITUTION

When Marc Blitzstein performed his playlet "Nickel under Your Foot" for Bertolt Brecht, Brecht asked Blitzstein to consider the prostitution beyond the literal prostitution of his central character, Moll. *The Cradle Will Rock* became an allegory for the "sellout of one's profession, one's talent, dignity, and integrity," according to Blitzstein.

While writing the screenplay, Brecht's challenge to Blitzstein became a thematic subtext for me, a lens through which every character is viewed at some point in the story. Susan Sarandon's Sarfatti and John Cusack's Rockefeller quite literally engage in the prostitution and destruction of art, while Ruben Blades's Rivera and Bill Murray's Crickshaw stay idealistically pure to their beliefs and are made to suffer the consequences. Vanessa Redgrave's Countess La Grange and Emily Watson's Olive reject the prostitution inherent in their personal relationships to participate in the performance at the Venice Theatre. The decisions of Aldo Silvano/Larry Foreman to perform/reject Mr. Mister's bribe represents those characters' choices to not prostitute themselves. They remain loyal to their beliefs while preserving their integrity and dignity. Their choices are made with great difficulty and risk.

How many of us when faced with this choice can honestly say we would risk economic security for our ideals? Just asking the question creates discomfort. I've talked to people who say they can't wait to sell

The enigmatic Mark Blitzstein, suddenly center stage. "I studied theatre history, and I never knew about this," says Hank Azaria. "It was the only production ever banned by the U.S. government. I thought Tim had made it up. I really did."

out. Life, with all its obstacles and difficulties, is hard enough without the added responsibility of pursuing idealistic purity.

The strong of heart who stand up and question, who remind us of our responsibility to mankind, are often made to pay a price for their actions. Indeed, Project 891 was dissolved after its renegade performance, and some of the actors were later blacklisted by the House Un-American Activities Committee in the fifties. But great inspiration also came from these struggles. Orson Welles would emerge as a director with unbounded creativity and brilliance. Marc Blitzstein would influence a generation of Broadway composers. Diego Rivera and Frida Kahlo would become two of the most revered artists of the twentieth century. And the Silvano boy who watches his father rise up in that theatre, what does he become? What grace and joy and dignity and common acts of heroism will he inspire?

CENSORSHIP

Censorship is a major theme in *Cradle Will Rock*. At the core of the film is this question: Should a government or benefactor have the right to determine the content of pieces of art that it commissions? In the film the character of Hearst says, "We support what we want art to be. We control the future of art because we pay for the future of art. Rather than starve, they'll adapt."

As I write this, an overly zealous mayor of a large municipality in America is embroiled in a battle with a museum over the content of an exhibition. At the heart of the controversy is the debate over whether public funds should be used to support art that the mayor finds objectionable. It seems to me a dangerous precedent to allow any politician's assessment of what constitutes legitimate art to determine what the public will see, and even more dangerous for a politician to be allowed to punish the artist or institution by withdrawing funding.

The victim of this calculated and dangerous dance with the First Amendment is freedom of expression, and ultimately, the cultural wealth of a nation.

Despite the implications of these headlines, I believe there are already too many artists who censor *themselves*. Why? Because they risk bad reviews, career stability, or being labeled didactic or overly intellectual. And that's where freedom suffers its most humiliating defeat—in conformity, self-censorship, deadening of thought, compliance with the status quo. Too often arts funding leads to benign art, theatre without teeth. Arts administrators learn quickly what kind of material will perpetuate funding and gradually leave behind courage and vision for convention and economic stability.

Hallie Flanagan left a template behind in her book, *Arena*. A rich, culturally vital, national theatre lies dormant. One can't get there without taking chances, getting one's hands dirty. It involves getting out of the cities and into the heartland, bringing plays that unsettle their audiences, that raise important questions and don't provide answers, that leave their audiences wanting to fight, argue, discuss. Our country would be the better for it—a stimulated, discerning, questioning public is the perfect citizenry in a democracy.

Ultimately this is why I did *Cradle Will Rock*. There is something deeply inspiring in the idealism and courage of artists from the thirties. To stand up in that theatre, to paint that mural, to risk your livelihood for your unshakeable belief in freedom of expression is an affirmation of life, of democracy, and of creativity. There will always be humorless, morally righteous people in government who will react negatively to courageous expression—one can only hope that their actions will create further inspiration for the artist. Out of the flames of controversy and oppression can come great work and unbridled expression.

Sources

American Social History Project. *Who Built America?* New York: Pantheon, 1992.

Benét, William Rose. *The Reader's Encyclopedia.* 2d ed. New York: Thomas Y. Crowell Co., 1965.

Buttita, Tony, and Barry Witham. *Uncle Sam Presents: A Memoir of the Federal Theatre, 1935–1939.* Philadelphia: University of Pennsylvania Press, 1982.

Cannistraro, Philip V., and Brian R. Sullivan. *Il Duce's Other Woman.* New York: William Morrow and Co., 1993.

Denning, Michael. *The Cultural Front.* New York: Verso, 1998.

DeNoon, Christopher. *Posters of the WPA.* Los Angeles: The Wheatley Press, 1987.

Ezor, Donna. *Jack, Orson and Uncle Sam: John Houseman and Orson Welles's Collaboration with the Federal Theatre Project 1935–1937.* Hunter College of the City of New York, 1999. Dissertation.

Flanagan, Hallie. *Arena.* New York: Limelight Editions, 1985.

Fuller, Peter. *Beyond the Crisis in Art.* London: Writers and Readers, 1982.

Galeano, Eduardo. *Memory of Fire, Vol. III, Memory of the Wind.* New York: Pantheon, 1988.

Gordon, Eric A. *Mark the Music: The Life and Work of Marc Blitzstein.* New York: St. Martin's Press, 1989.

Jackson, Kenneth T. *The Encyclopedia of New York City.* New Haven: Yale University Press, 1995.

Kazacoff, George. *Dangerous Theatre: The Federal Theatre Project as a Forum for New Plays.* New York: Peter Lang, 1989.

Langer, William L., Ed. *Western Civilization.* New York: American Heritage, 1968.

O'Connor, John, and Lorraine Brown, Eds. *Free, Adult, Uncensored: A Living History of the Federal Theatre Project.* Washington, D.C.: New Republic Books, 1978.

Parenti, Michael. *Blackshirts and Reds: Rational Fascism and the Overthrow of Communism.* San Francisco: City Lights Books, 1997.

Quita, Craig E. *Black Drama of the Federal Theatre Era.* Amherst: University of Massachusetts Press, 1980.

Ribner, Irving. *Christopher Marlowe's* Dr. Faustus: *Text and Major Criticism.* New York: The Odyssey Press, 1966.

Rivera, Diego. *My Art, My Life.* New York: Dover Publications, 1991.

Sporn, Paul. *Against Itself: The Federal Theatre and Writers' Projects in the Midwest.* Detroit: Wayne State University Press, 1995.

Taylor, A. J. P., and J. M. Roberts, Eds. *Purnell's History of the 20th Century.* New York: Purnell, 1971.

Time-Life Books. *Hard Times: The 30s.* Our American Century series. Alexandria, Va: Time-Life Books, 1998.

Trager, James. *The People's Chronology.* New York: Holt Rhinehart Winston, 1979.

Tue, Liang Tee. *The Mirror and the Reflections.* Hunter College of the City of New York, 1989. Dissertation.

Watkins, T. H. *The Great Depression: America in the 1930s.* Boston: Little, Brown and Co., 1993.

Welles, Orson, and Peter Bogdanovich. *This Is Orson Welles.* New York: HarperCollins, 1992.

Williams, Jay. *Stage Left.* New York: Charles Scribner's Sons, 1974.

Zinn, Howard. *The Twentieth Century: A People's History.* New York: HarperCollins, 1998.

Acknowledgments

The author would like to thank the staff at Havoc for their research and contributions to this book, including Chris Talbott and Ruben Carbajal. My assistants, Allison Hebble and Nadia Benamara, have both been indispensable to this project.

Special thanks to the Disney team of Mae Joyce, Holly Clark, and Karen Glass, as well as to the contributors Eric Darton, Nancy Stearns Bercaw, and Robert Tracy. The photographers Demi Todd and David Lee have supplied terrific images of *Cradle Will Rock* for this volume.

A million thanks to Lorraine Brown and George Mason University, where the Federal Theatre Archive is located in their Fenwick Library Collection.

Additional thanks go to Marc Blitzstein's heirs, Stephen Davis and Christopher Davis; Bertolt Brecht's daughter, Barbara Brecht-Schall; Susan Sarandon; Eva Amurri; and my two sons, Jack and Miles.

Finally, I would like to thank my publisher, Esther Margolis, her staff at Newmarket Press, and, in particular, editor Theresa Burns, designer Timothy Shaner, production director Frank DeMaio, and coordinator Elyse Cogan, for making this book a reality.

The publisher would like to thank our skillful editor, Theresa Burns, for her unflagging commitment to this very demanding project; the talented Timothy Shaner, for his outstanding design sensibility; Elyse Cogan, for her invaluable assistance in photo research; and, for their editorial and production help throughout, Frank DeMaio, Dorothy Gribbin, Tom Perry, Todd Sinclair, and Christopher Measom. Very special thanks to Nadia Benamara at Havoc for being our "connector" to all the necessary people and materials whenever and whatever. We are grateful for the cooperation of Karen Glass, Mae Joyce, and Holly Clark at Disney; production designer, Richard Hoover, who lent us his extraordinary research notebooks; and Lorraine Brown at George Mason University, without whose efforts the work of the Federal Theatre may never have been brought fully to light, as well as the staff at Fenwick Library, especially Robert Vay, for help with archival photographs. Thanks to Eric Darton, Nancy Stearns Bercaw, and Robert Tracy for their editorial contributions and Paul Newman for his Foreword.

And, most of all, we'd like to thank Tim Robbins, whose dedication to this film, and the history behind it, inspired us all.

Archival Photo Credits

THE CAST

Marc Blitzstein . . . . HANK AZARIA
Diego Rivera . . . . RUBEN BLADES
Hazel Huffman . . . . JOAN CUSACK
Nelson Rockefeller . . . . JOHN CUSACK
John Houseman . . . . CARY ELWES
Gray Mathers . . . . PHILIP BAKER HALL
Hallie Flanagan . . . . CHERRY JONES
Orson Welles . . . . ANGUS MACFADYEN
Tommy Crickshaw . . . . BILL MURRAY
Countess La Grange . . . . VANESSA REDGRAVE
Margherita Sarfatti . . . . SUSAN SARANDON
John Adair . . . . JAMEY SHERIDAN
Aldo Silvano . . . . JOHN TURTURRO
Olive Stanton . . . . EMILY WATSON

Harry Hopkins . . . . BOB BALABAN
Sid . . . . JACK BLACK
Larry . . . . KYLE GASS
Carlo . . . . PAUL GIAMATTI
Frank Marvel . . . . BARNARD HUGHES
Sophie Silvano . . . . BARBARA SUKOWA

MAXINE ELLIOTT'S

Dulce Fox . . . . VICTORIA CLARK
Sandra Mescal . . . . ERIN HILL
Will Geer . . . . DANIEL JENKINS
Bert Weston . . . . TIMOTHY JEROME
Canada Lee . . . . CHRIS McKINNEY
Hiram Sherman . . . . HENRY STRAM

Augusta Weissberger . . . . ADELE ROBBINS
Abe Feder . . . . LEE ARENBERG
George Zorn . . . . ALLAN NICHOLLS
National Guardsman . . . . ROB CARLSON
Reporter . . . . ALISON TATLOCK
Lucille Schly . . . . DINA PLATIAS
Alma Dixon . . . . PAM HENRY

Stagehand . . . . EMMA SMITH STEVENS

Lehman Engel . . . . STEVEN TYLER
Accordion . . . . CHARLES GIORDANO
Trumpet . . . . JEFFREY KIEVIT
Trombone . . . . KENNETH FINN
Clarinet . . . . KENNETH HITCHCOCK
Alto Saxophone . . . . DAVID D'ANGELO
Percussion . . . . DAVID RATAJCZAK

FEDERAL THEATRE

Donald O'Hara . . . . STEPHEN SPINELLA
Rose . . . . BRENDA PRESSLEY
Pierre De Rohan . . . . BRIAN BROPHY
Beaver Man . . . . DAVID COSTABILE
Beaver Woman . . . . MARLA SCHAFFEL
Beaver Accordion Accompanist . . . . . .DOMINIC CORTESE

POWER

William Randolph Hearst . . . . JOHN CARPENTER
Marion Davies . . . . GRETCHEN MOL
Congressman Starnes . . . . GIL ROBBINS
Chairman Martin Dies . . . . HARRIS YULIN
Paul Edwards . . . . NED BELLAMY
James . . . . V. J. FOSTER

Butler . . . . WILLIAM DUELL
Tailor . . . . ALBERT MACKLIN
Reporter . . . . SCOTT SOWERS
Reporter . . . . BOBBY AMORE

SILVANO

Mama . . . . LYNN COHEN
Papa . . . . DOMINIC CHIANESE
Uncle . . . . PETER JACOBSON
Joey . . . . EVAN KATZ
Chance . . . . ALYSIA ZUCKER
Giovanna . . . . SARAH HYLAND
Marta . . . . STEPHANIE ROTH

VAUDEVILLE

Melvin . . . . SPANKY McHUGH
Puppeteer . . . . TODD STOCKMAN
Vaudeville Theater Manager . . . . . . PATRICK HUSTED
Plate Twirler . . . . JAY GREEN
Assistant Plate Twirler . . . . CAROLYN WEST

BLITZSTEIN

Bertolt Brecht . . . . STEVEN SKYBELL
Eva Blitzstein . . . . SUSAN HEIMBINDER
"Joe Worker" Singer . . . . AUDRA McDONALD
Liberty Committee #1 . . . . ROBERT ARI
Liberty Committee #2 . . . . MICHELE PAWK
Dream Larry Foreman . . . . GREGG EDELMAN
Dream Cop . . . . MATTHEW BENNETT

ROCKEFELLER CENTER

Aide . . . . BRIAN POWELL
Lawyer . . . . JACK WILLIS
Mendez . . . . GILBERT CRUZ
Sol . . . . ROBERT HIRSCHFELD
Guard . . . . P. J. BROWN
Protester . . . . MICHAEL RIVKIN
Protester . . . . KEIRA NAUGHTON
Claire . . . . TAYLOR STANLEY
Pete . . . . TOMMY ALLEN
Mendez Double . . . . JEFF BUTCHER
Sol Double . . . . SANDY HAMILTON

DIEGO

Frida Kahlo . . . . CORINA KATT
Models . . . . JOSIE WHITTLESEY
SANDRA LINDQUIST
TAMIKA LAMISON

OPENING

Worker In Theatre . . . . EDWARD JAMES HYLAND
Man on Street . . . . BORIS McGIVER

WPA

Carpenter . . . . CHRIS BAUER
Man in Line . . . . LEONARDO CIMINO
Clerk . . . . PATTI TIPPO
Administrator . . . . CARRIE PRESTON
Disgruntled Workers . . . . MARY ROBBINS
CHRISTOPHER TALBOTT
SUSAN BRUCE
IAN BAGG

RIOT

Carl Jasper . . . . TONY AMENDOLA
Stunt Coordinator . . . . JERY HEWITT

THE CREW

Written and Directed by . . . . .TIM ROBBINS

Produced by . . . . JON KILIK
TIM ROBBINS
LYDIA DEAN PILCHER

Executive Producers . . . . LOUISE KRAKOWER
FRANK BEACHAM
ALLAN NICHOLS

Director of Photography . . . . JEAN YVES ESCOFFIER

Production Design . . . . RICHARD HOOVER

Editor . . . . GERALDINE PERONI

Costume Design . . . . RUTH MYERS

With Songs by . . . . MARC BLITZSTEIN

Music . . . . DAVID ROBBINS

Casting . . . . DOUG AIBEL

Unit Production Manager . . . . AMY HERMAN

First Assistant Director . . . . ALLAN NICHOLLS

Second Assistant Director . . . . DANIELLE RIGBY

Associate Producer . . . . ALLISON HEBBLE

Sound Mixer . . . . TOD A. MAITLAND, C.A.S

Camera Operator . . . . JIM McCONKEY
Script Supervisor . . . . EVA Z. CABRERA
Supervising Art Director . . . . TROY SIZEMORE
Set Decorator . . . . DEBRA SCHUTT
Property Master . . . . TOMMY ALLEN

Make-Up Design and Supervision . . . . MICHAL BIGGER
Hair Design and Supervision . . . . PEG SCHIERHOLZ

Art Director . . . . PETER ROGNESS
Assistant Art Director . . . . BARBRA MATIS
Assistant Art Director . . . . ADAM SCHER
Leadman . . . . RICHARD TICE

Key Make-Up . . . . LINDA GRIMES
Key Hairstylist . . . . KATHE SWANSON
Hairstylists . . . . MILTON A. BURAS
JAQUELINE PAYNE
DALE BROWNELL
JERRY OZCARLO
Make-Up Artists . . . . EVA POLYWKA
LYNN CAMPBELL
GLORIA GRANT

First Assistant Camera . . . . BOBBY MANCUSO
Second Assistant Camera . . . . CHRISTIAN CARMODY
Camera Loader . . . . SCOTT MAGUIRE
First Boom Operator . . . . MICHAEL SCOTT
Second Boom Operator-Utility . . . . . FRANK J. GRAZIADEI
Multi-track Recordist . . . . THOMAS GOULD
Recordist . . . . T. J. O'MARA

Gaffer . . . . MICHAEL J. DELANEY
Best Boy Electric . . . . PETR HLINOMAZ
Best Boy Rigging Electric . . . . CHRISTOPHER DOLAN

Company Electrics . . . . MICHAEL McDONALD
XAVIER HENSELMANN
JOSEPH BACCARI
TOM LANDI
SCOTT GREGOIRE
KEVIN FITZPATRICK

Key Grip . . . . BILLY MILLER
Best Boy Grip . . . . MICHAEL BETZAG
Dolly Grip . . . . KURT RIMMEL
Company Grips . . . . DAMIEN DONOHUE
CHRISTOPHER VALENTINO
Rigging Gaffer . . . . BOB McGAVIN
Key Rigging Grip . . . . CRAIG VACCARO
Best Boy Rigging Grip . . . . NICK VACCARO

Construction Coordinator . . . . KENNETH D. NELSON
Construction Foreman . . . . STEVEN E. LAWLER
Lead Foreman . . . . JOHN R. JOHNSTON
Key Construction Grip . . . . PETER BETULIA
Lead Construction Grip . . . . ADAM NOVICH
Lead Scenic . . . . ROBERT TOPOL
Camera Scenic . . . . M. TONY TROTTA

Choreographer . . . . ROB MARSHALL
Associate Choreographer . . . . CYNTHIA ONRUBIA
Dialect Coach . . . . TIM MONICH

Extras Casting . . . . BYRON CRYSTAL

Post Production Supervisor . . . . KELLEY CRIBBEN
Additional Editor . . . . JAMES KWEI
First Assistant Editor . . . . MISAKO SHIMIZU
Second Assistant Editor . . . . IAN SILVERSTEIN
Assistant Editor . . . . SARA THORSON
Apprentice Editor . . . . V. RENEE TAYLOR
Post Production Assistants . . . . NEIL A. STELZNER
ELAINE GARTNER

Prop masters and MVPs Sandy Hamilton and Tommy Allen.

Supervising Sound Editor . . . . ELIZA PALEY
ADR Editor . . . . JANE McCULLEY
Dialogue Editors . . . . JEFFREY STERN
TONY MARTINEZ
SYLVIA MENNO
Supervising Sound F/X Editor . . . . WARREN SHAW
Sound F/X Editor . . . . BRUCE KITZMEYER
Assistant Sound Editors . . . . BRIAN LANGMAN
AJAE CLEARWAY
Assistant ADR Editor . . . . BARRY MALAWSKI
Apprentice Sound Editor . . . . GREGG GETHERALL
Systems Engineer, Planet 10 Post . . . . ROLAND VAJS
Sound Editorial Intern . . . . LUKE THORPE
Supervising Foley Editor . . . . BRUCE PROSS
Foley Editor . . . . FRANK KERN
Foley Artist . . . . MARKO COSTANZO
ADR Engineer . . . . DAVID BOULTON
Audio Post Production Services . . . PLANET 10 POST, INC

Assistant Set Decorator . . . . KARIN WIESEL
On Set Dressers . . . . JOANN ATWOOD
REBECCA MEIS
Set Dressers . . . . JOAN FINLAY
JAMES ARCHER
PHILIP CANFIELD
KEVIN BLAKE
RUTH DELEON
CONRAD BRINK
JEFF BRINK
KELLY CANFIELD
DEBORAH CANFIELD
PATRICE LONGO
MARK NEWELL
SARAH FREDERICKS

Seven Deadly Sins Puppet Designer . . . MATTHEW OWENS

Assistant Property Master . . . . SANDY HAMILTON
Property Assistant . . . . ANN EDGEWORTH
Researcher . . . . KATHRYN M. RICHARDS
Special Effects Coordinator . . . . J. C. BROTHERHOOD

Production Coordinator . . . . DIANA E. LATHAM
Assistant Production
   Coordinator . . . . CHRISTINE V. DESROCHERS
Production Secretary . . . . NICOLE TAVENNER
Second Second Assistant Director . . . . SHEA ROWAN
Additional Second Assistant Director . . . SUSAN PERLMAN
DGA Trainee . . . . KATHRYN SHERTZER
Havoc Manager . . . . CHRISTOPHER TALBOTT
Assistant to Tim Robbins . . . . NADIA BENAMARA

Location Manager . . . . BRYAN THOMAS
Assistant Location Manager . . . . CAREY DEPALMA
Location Assistants . . . . KELLIE MORRISON
TYSON BIDNER
DEMIAN RESNICK
DEAN STEPHENS

Production Accountant . . . . MARA HADE CONNOLLY
Assistant Auditor . . . . JODI SHAPERA YEAGER
Assistant Accountant . . . . JESSICA JOHNSON
Payroll . . . . JORGE AGUIRRE

146

Assistant Costume Designer . . . . FRANK FLEMING
Costume Assistant . . . . ALIX HESTER
Costume Supervisors . . . . LISA FRUCHT
DAVID DUMAIS
Assistant Costume Supervisors . . . . SUSAN J. WRIGHT
BARRETT HONG
Costumer . . . . AMY HABACKER

Art Department Administrator . . . . ERIN W. SIBLEY
Assistant to the Production Designer . . . . . TINA KHAYAT
Construction Office Coordinator . . . NICOLE DUCHARME

Key Production Assistant . . . . DOUG PLASSE

Production Assistants . . . . JESSE NYE
PEGGY ROBINSON
ADAM WEISINGER
ANDREA O'CONNOR
MICHAEL G. MOORADIAN
SABRINA A. HAMADY
AUTUMN SAVILLE
NICOLE KLETT
EDDIE ROCHE
HEIDI PIEH
Unit Publicist . . . . . . NANCY SELTZER AND ASSOCIATES
Publicist . . . . MARA BUXBAUM

Still Photographers . . . . DEMMIE TODD
DAVID LEE

Transportation Captain . . . . JAMES WHALEN
Transportation Co-Captain . . . . TIM SHANNON
Casting Assistant . . . . JORDAN BESWICK
Extras Casting Associate . . . . DAVID MOY
Extras Casting Assistants . . . . KEISHA AMES
PHILIP VANSCOTIER

Re-Recording Mixers . . . . LEE DICHTER
REILLY STEELE
Re-Recorded at . . . . SOUND ONE CORP.
Titles Designed and Produced by . . . . BALSMEYER &
EVERETT, INC.
Negative Cutter . . . . J.G. FILMS, INC.
Dailies Advisor . . . . JOE VIOLANTE
Color Timer . . . . DON CIANA
Post Accounting . . . . MICHELLE GEBERT
Storyboard Artist . . . . KARL SHEFELMAN
Video Playback . . . . KEVIN McKENNA
Theatrical Lighting Designer . . . . BRIAN MACDEVITT
Ventriloquist Consultants . . . . TODD STOCKMAN
ALAN SEMOCK
Caterer . . . . REEL FOODS
Craft Service . . . . BY DAWN'S EARLY LIGHT
DAWN, NIR, DAVID
Production Intern . . . . KIP MEYERS
Background Vocals . . DAVID KRAMER'S LOOPING GROUP

Music Supervisor . . . . DAVID ROBBINS

Score Orchestrated & Conducted by . . . DAVID CAMPBELL
Score Arrangements . . . . DAVID ROBBINS
and DAVID CAMPBELL
Music Preparation . . . . BETTIE ROSS-BLUMER
Blitzstein Music Conducted by . . . . STEVEN TYLER
Music Editor . . . . DANIEL LIEBERSTEIN

Musicians' Contractor and Coordinator . . JULIET HAFFNER
Assistant Music Editor . . . . DEBRA VICTOROFF
Music Scoring Mixer . . . . GARY CHESTER
Recording Assistants . . . . YVONNE YEDIBALIAN
JIM MURRAY
Recorded and Mixed at . . . . EDISON STUDIO, N.Y.C
Executive in Charge of Music for The
Buena Vista Motion Pictures Group . . . KATHY NELSON

THE MUSICIANS
Piano . . . . STEVEN TYLER
Violin Soloist . . . . ANDREW BIRD
Clarinet Soloist . . . . PAQUITO D'RIVERA

Reproductions of Diego Rivera and Frida Kahlo
Artworks Authorized by DOLORES OLMEDO PATINO
and INSTITUTO NACIONAL DE
BELLAS ARTES Y LITERATURA
Additional Artwork
Permissions by . . . . ARTISTS RIGHTS SOCIETY
Images of Art Provided by . . . . ART RESOURCE
Stock Footage Provided by . . . . ARCHIVE FILMS

Excerpt from "A Man Young and Old"
by William Butler Yeats

Dialogue in Dies Committee Hearings
taken directly from Congressional Record

Produced in Association with
KRAKOWER/BEACHAM PRODUCTIONS

SPECIAL THANKS
Joe Roth, Elaine Goldsmith-Thomas, Sam Cohn,
Bart Walker, Geoffrey Ammer, Oren Aviv, Mae Joyce,
Iya Labunka, John Sable, Nadine Hasan,
Fortunata & Fortunato Federico

IN MEMORIAM
Rick Dior, Barton Heyman, Sam Fuller

This film was edited on old-fashioned machines.

Prints by TECHNICOLOR® Color by TECHNICOLOR®
Filmed in PANAVISION®

Produced & Distributed on EASTMAN FILM

THIS PICTURE MADE UNDER
THE JURISDICTION OF

AFFILIATED WITH
A.F.L.-C.I.O.-C.L.C.

FOR LES TOMALIN

Distributed by BUENA VISTA PICTURES DISTRIBUTION